KNIGHTMASTER

ORONIS KNIGHTS
BOOK 1

ANNA HACKETT

Knightmaster

Published by Anna Hackett

Copyright 2023 by Anna Hackett

Cover by Ana Cruz Arts

Edits by Tanya Saari

ISBN (ebook): 978-1-922414-78-6

ISBN (paperback): 978-1-922414-79-3

WHAT READERS ARE SAYING ABOUT ANNA'S ACTION ROMANCE

Heart of Eon - Romantic Book of the Year (Ruby) winner 2020

Cyborg - PRISM Award Winner 2019

Edge of Eon and Mission: Her Protection - Romantic Book of the Year (Ruby) finalists 2019

Unfathomed and Unmapped - Romantic Book of the Year (Ruby) finalists 2018

Unexplored – Romantic Book of the Year (Ruby) Novella Winner 2017

Return to Dark Earth – One of Library Journal's Best E-Original Books for 2015 and two-time SFR Galaxy Awards winner

At Star's End – One of Library Journal's Best E-Original Romances for 2014

The Phoenix Adventures – SFR Galaxy Award Winner for Most Fun New Series and "Why Isn't This a Movie?" Series

Beneath a Trojan Moon – SFR Galaxy Award Winner and RWAus Ella Award Winner

Hell Squad – SFR Galaxy Award for best Post-Apocalypse for Readers who don't like Post-Apocalypse

"Like Indiana Jones meets Star Wars. A treasure hunt with a steamy romance." – SFF Dragon, review of *Among Galactic Ruins*

"Action, danger, aliens, romance – yup, it's another great book from Anna Hackett!" – Book Gannet Reviews, review of *Hell Squad: Marcus*

Sign up for my VIP mailing list and get your *free box set* containing three action-packed romances.

Visit here to get started: www.annahackett.com

CHAPTER ONE

"How much longer?"

"One hour until we reach orbit around Oron, Sub-Captain."

"Thanks, Ensign." Sub-Captain Kennedy Black nodded at the young man. Then she leaned in and pulled a small candy out of her pocket. "Here's that Eon candy I promised that you'd love. I loaded the recipe into the ship's food printers."

"Oh." The ensign's eyes lit up. "Thanks, Kennedy." He quickly pocketed the small treat.

Kennedy straightened with a wink, then turned to stare out the wide viewscreen into the blackness of space. The *Helios* was the pride of the Space Corps' fleet. It was the latest design, containing new-generation tech, with some very experimental alien technology built into it.

It made her fast and dangerous. Plus, it had a new stealth mode that was being tested on this trip. So, the *Helios* could be sneaky, as well. Kennedy was pretty pleased she'd been able to hitch a ride on her.

The rock-solid alliance that Earth had formed with the Eon warriors over the last year and a half had really paid off. Eon and Earth scientists now worked together, sharing information, learning from each other.

God, it had been a dream come true for a xenoanthropologist like Kennedy and the other members of Space Corps Exploration Division. They'd spent endless hours poring over the information on the Eon Empire, plus other planets and species the Eon had documented.

There were a few times she hadn't slept for a day or two because she'd been so lost in absorbing everything she could. She'd taken several stim shots just so she could stay awake.

Earth had definitely benefited from the new alliance. It helped immensely that the Eon King had fallen head over heels for a woman from Earth. Kennedy shook her head. It was hard to believe that Captain Alea Rodriguez was now a *queen*. Kennedy was friendly with the sharp, dedicated woman.

For a second, Kennedy just stared into the void through the view screen. She knew some people hated the emptiness.

She didn't.

She saw the adventure, the endless possibilities.

Her pulse did a little skitter. Shaking her head again, she swiveled and straightened her navy-blue Space Corps uniform. Around her, the bridge of the ship was busy, but calm. The *Helios'* crew was excellent, and each member was focused on their jobs. Captain Margo Attaway ran a tight ship, and it helped that she'd gotten to choose the best of the best to man the *Helios*.

Kennedy headed off the bridge, on her way to inform her charges that they were almost at their destination.

She found them on the observation deck. Ambassador Douglas James was a tall, stately man, with steel-gray hair, and a long, patrician face. He was to be Earth's new ambassador to the Oronis. His small, curvy, blonde wife stood beside him. The Frenchwoman was the opposite of her husband. Claudine was bubbly, a little raunchy, and had a hell of a sense of humor. Kennedy liked her immensely.

But it was the couple standing beside them that caught Kennedy's full attention.

The man was hard to ignore. War Commander Davion Thann-Eon was big, muscular, and in Kennedy's opinion, total eye candy. His sleeveless, black outfit showed off his brawny arms. The man was outrageously fit. He had a rugged face, framed by longish brown hair that curled at his collar.

But it was the fact that he was clearly besotted with his wife that made him even more attractive.

Eve Thann-Eon, formally Sub-Captain Eve Traynor, was something of a legend at Space Corps. She'd had a colorful career, and was a tough woman with a reputation for taking risks and never backing down from a fight.

One risk—abducting an alien war commander—had clearly paid off.

The woman's two sisters were also now mated to Eon warriors, as well. Yep, the Traynor sisters were all legends. The women who'd dared to abduct an Eon warrior, steal from the Eon, and hijack one of their warships.

The fit brunette grinned at her husband, then smiled down at the small, seven-month-old boy currently tucked securely in his father's strong arms and fast asleep.

Jeez, just another thing to add to the man's hotness factor.

Not that Kennedy needed a man. Her focus was solely on her career for about a hundred different reasons, the top of the list being her thirst to see beyond the borders of Earth's solar system.

There was *so* much out there to see and discover.

Eve spotted her. "Kennedy. Are we almost there?"

"We are." Kennedy crossed the room. "We have one hour until we enter orbit around Oron."

"Excellent." Eve's eyes twinkled. "I cannot wait to see the Oronis homeworld."

Kennedy was vibrating with excitement. The Oronis were *knights*. Fierce fighters dedicated to their queen, and a creed of honor and duty.

"I'm intrigued as well," Douglas said. "We know so little about them."

"They're excellent fighters, good allies, and honorable," Davion said, keeping his deep voice low so he didn't wake his sleeping son.

Eve rolled her eyes. "Spoken like a warrior."

Kennedy smiled. "Douglas, I dug up some notes on Oronis politics for you from our Eon archives. I sent it to your communicator."

The ambassador straightened. "Wonderful. Thanks, Kennedy."

Claudine cocked a hip. "Kennedy, you are a wonder. This entire trip, whatever we've needed, you've found it."

"That's my job."

"*Non*, I think it is you. Your special superpower." The woman twirled a finger. "So, what do you have for me today?"

Kennedy grinned. "How about some lavender-infused lotion? I made it up last night when you said the air recyclers were drying out your hands."

Claudine's eyes widened. "French lavender?"

"*Mais oui.* I'll drop it by your cabin later."

Claudine turned to the others. "It's a superpower, I tell you."

"Let's hope it helps convince the Oronis to sign an alliance with Earth." Eve met Kennedy's gaze. "It really is an honor to be invited to attend the knightqueen's ball. I know they weren't certain about including Earth."

No, the Oronis tended to stick to themselves, protecting their quadrant of space fiercely. But Eve, Alea, and some other Space Corps members—who'd worked with the Eon warriors to help Earth repel an attack from a nasty insectoid species, the Kantos—had made a good impression on the Oronis.

Hence the invite to the planet Oron for the knightqueen's ball.

And for Douglas to possibly become the new ambassador between Earth and Oron.

Kennedy was here to make sure it all ran smoothly. She was acting as chief liaison for the group, in addition to documenting everything she could about the Oronis culture.

Her boss in the Exploration Division at Space Corps had told her not to screw it up. She was part manager, part xenoanthropologist, part assistant, part security. Excitement licked at her. She wanted to be part of the new exploration teams being put together by Space Corps. With the new tech they'd gained from the Eon, they could go farther, explore new worlds, document new species. Her chest filled with a bubble of excitement.

God, if only her parents could see her now.

But, as her boss liked to tell her, tact and diplomacy were not always Kennedy's strongest skills.

No, often she became rather focused on her work, and she wasn't afraid to sometimes bend the rules. Just a teeny bit. When it made sense, of course.

Her parents had been renowned archeologists, and had taught her that adventuring into new places meant being adaptable, pivoting when needed, and that sometimes, old rules no longer applied to strange, new situations.

She felt a pang in her chest. They'd been so passionate about their work, and each other. Sometimes, she'd felt she was at the bottom of their list of priorities, but she'd always loved hearing about their digs and adventures. She still had the collection of letters and cards they used to send her from wherever they were in the world. As a little girl at home with her nanny, she'd cherished every exciting word and picture.

It had been a sign that they were at least thinking about her.

They'd died years ago in a terrible sandstorm on a desert expedition. She still missed them, but was grateful they'd died together.

"Do you have a dress to wear to the ball, Kennedy?"

Eve wrinkled her nose. "I don't love dressing up, but I'm told it's a bit of a thing on Oronis. The theme is all black and white."

"Ball gowns are *not* my thing," Kennedy replied. "Give me a Space Corps uniform and a pair of boots any day."

Evie smiled. "Comfy boots."

The women laughed and Kennedy enjoyed the camaraderie. She liked Eve a lot.

"I was told a suitable dress was included for me." Kennedy waved a hand. "I'm certain it'll be fine." And hopefully plain enough for her to fade into the background. She wanted *to* observe, not *be* observed. Plus, she was there to keep her charges safe and happy.

It was important to make a good impression on the Oronis. To forge an alliance that would give Earth access to more technology, knowledge, and allies. She was very keen to see the Oronis knights up close. They were all highly trained, and dedicated to the knightqueen.

Kennedy found the whole thing fascinating.

The doors to the observation deck opened, and a small, metallic ball—just a little larger than a baseball—zoomed inside. Kennedy's lips twitched. The small drone whirled around them, then hovered behind her head, near her left ear.

Eve smiled. "I was about to ask you where your shadow was."

"Beep was no doubt exploring the ship, and flirting with the main computer." Kennedy held up her hand and the drone nuzzled her palm. He made a few loud beeps. He wasn't really a *he*, but that was how she thought of her drone. He was part communicator, part computer, part weapon.

He was part of a now-obsolete program—all the other drones of his type had been decommissioned—but Beep was...different. And he'd claimed Kennedy as his.

Suddenly, baby Kane's eyes popped open. He saw his father and grinned with four white teeth. Kennedy watched the big warrior's face soften. The little boy had the same blue-black eyes as his father.

"There's my boy," Davion murmured.

Kane made a sound, then saw his mother. His grin widened.

"Such a happy child," Claudine murmured.

"Because mommy and daddy are always taking you exciting places." Eve took her son and nuzzled his chubby cheek.

Kennedy wondered what it would have been like to travel with her parents. They'd always told her it was too dangerous.

Kane spotted Beep, who he was fascinated with, and waved a hand. Beep backed up and slipped behind Kennedy's back.

"Coward," she murmured. Poor Beep had gotten close to baby Kane once on the trip. Once had been enough for the drone. Kane had a surprisingly strong grip.

Kennedy pulled a small toy from her pocket. The rattle was made to look like an Eon sword.

"Oh, that's so cute," Eve said.

Kane snatched the toy and shook it. Delight crossed his face.

"Look, there's Oron," Davion said.

Kennedy swiveled and sucked in a breath.

Wow. Just...wow.

The planet was mostly green, covered in bands of cloud, with large bodies of water visible. They were all a deep blue with a tinge of purple.

"Take a few pictures for me, Beep."

The drone whirred, capturing images that would download straight to Kennedy's database. Then Beep made a noise and bumped gently against her head.

"Me too, Beep. I'm very excited to see Oron."

Her chest expanded with that feeling she got whenever she was going somewhere new. Excitement, anticipation, but this time, it was mixed with a sense of something big.

Like something important was on the horizon.

"I WANT extra patrols on the eastern wall."

"Yes, Knightmaster."

"And tell the knightguards we'll need more guards at the ballroom entrances for the Grand Hall," Knightmaster Ashtin Caydor ordered.

"I'll coordinate with the Captain of the Queen's Knightguards."

"Thank you, Meric."

The young knight straightened, bowed his head, and strode off.

Ashtin turned, standing at the balcony railing on the

lower levels of the palace. The city of Aravena—the capital of Oron—spread out before him.

The Castle Aravena was the center of the city, perched on the wide, purple waters of the River Camlann. He always felt an immense sense of pride looking at the shining city.

The castle had several spires of different heights, all in gleaming-white stone and blue glass. The main tower was a blade shape, covered in sparkling windows. The lower levels were wide tiers, filled with greenery and gardens.

There were other tall buildings in the city, spearing high into the sky, but most of the city was filled with smaller buildings, homes, and structures, along with the graceful arches of the many bridges that crossed the river.

He'd grown up here. He lived a life dedicated to his planet, his people, and his knightqueen.

He'd come from nothing, become a knight, and he held the code of knighthood as the cornerstone of his being.

He'd die for Oronis, die for his queen.

And he didn't like the idea of this ball.

Ashtin scowled. The Eon were coming, which he didn't mind. They were the strongest allies of the Oronis.

But there were also delegates from Phidea V, Borus, Xerus, and...Earth.

Ashtin glanced over toward the spaceport at the edge of the city. He didn't know these other species well, especially the Terrans from Earth. He'd fought alongside several fighters from Earth with the Eon. The King of the Eon had married one.

But what Ashtin had since learned of Earth made him wary. It was a messy, chaotic world that was still finding its place in the universe. And not all of the planet's people had honor.

He wasn't certain he could trust them.

He definitely wasn't sure about inviting them into the heart of Oron.

Especially when the worst enemy of the Oronis were rumbling.

The Gek'Dragar.

He gripped the stone railing under his hands and squeezed.

The Gek'Dragar and the Oronis had been enemies for centuries. The brutal wars of Gammis III had seen many knights die in battle to stop the enemy species overrunning Oronis space.

The Oronis still sang of the victories and losses to this day.

Defeated, the Gek'Dragar had retreated well past Oronis' distant borders. For centuries, they'd heard nothing of the other species.

But now, they were surfacing again.

There were reports of disturbing attacks along the border. Attacks on Oronis ships and small outposts.

Ashtin swiveled and walked inside the castle, his boots clicking on the shiny floor made from rich, Camlann marble in the purest white.

He would *not* let the Gek'Dragar hurt his people. He and the other knights would use all of their abilities to fight, serve, and protect the knightqueen and the Oronis.

He strode up a wide sweep of stairs, and then down a long corridor.

Ahead, two of the queen's personal knightguards flanked an ornate door. They nodded to him, and then the door slid open.

He was met by the queen's captain of the guards, Knightguard Sten Carahan. The big man nodded.

Sten was older than Ashtin by about ten years, and had been with the queen's guards since she was a teenager. He was battle hardened, and would die for her.

Just as Ashtin would. The knightqueen was the beating heart of the Oronis.

Most Oronis were tall and lean, with pure-black hair like Ashtin's, or pure blonde like the knightqueen, and had blue eyes. Sten was different. He was tall, but broad, and had rugged features and brown hair he cut ruthlessly short. His eyes were a dark green. One cheek was covered in scars he'd gotten when protecting the queen from an attack, years ago. He'd been injured keeping her safe from an alien *nelok*. The vicious creatures had long claws, and one had slashed him badly. Sten had protected the queen for two days, and his wounds had become infected. By the time they'd been rescued, his wounds hadn't been able to be fully healed by the knighthealers.

Sten didn't care. He'd once told Ashtin that they made him scarier, and helped him keep the knightqueen safer.

"Ashtin." The man's voice was a low, deep growl.

"Sten."

"How does security look for this *gul*-vexed ball?"

Clearly Sten was even less happy about the ball than Ashtin. "Good. We'll increase patrols and guards."

The knightguard nodded and paced away. "We have too many unknown people from planets we don't know anything about." The man scowled and crossed his brawny arms. He looked like he could've had some Eon blood in him. "I don't like it."

"I don't either, but Knightqueen Carys wouldn't budge. She wants to forge new alliances." Ashtin put his hands on his hips. "Perhaps that's not a bad thing with the rumbles coming from the Gek'Dragar."

Now, Sten's scowl turned fierce. "If the Gek'Dragar step one foot on Oron, or go anywhere near the queen, I'll slaughter the lot of them. They are *not* getting close to her. Never again."

There was death in the man's voice.

It had been a Gek'Dragar assassin, who'd killed the previous knightqueen and her consort. The assassin had almost killed the then-Princess Carys.

Ashtin knew just how dedicated Sten was.

The click of heels on the floor had them both turning.

Knightqueen Carys smiled. "Hello, Ashtin."

"Your Highness." He bowed his head.

She was tall and slim, with long, platinum-colored hair. She had a stunningly beautiful face, but he'd seen her fight—she was skilled and powerful. Today, she wore a black, sleeveless dress that emphasized her tiny waist, and had two long slits in the skirt. Beneath, she wore black boots that reached to her mid-thighs.

"How are preparations for the ball?" she asked.

"Progressing," Ashtin replied. "I've suggested some increased security measures—"

She rolled her gold eyes—a sign of her royal lineage. "You sound like Sten."

Her knightguard grunted.

"I do not think the delegations from our allied planets will cause any problems. Good relations take trust."

"And trust takes time," Sten countered.

She touched the guard's arm. "Yes, but we must take the first steps some time."

"The people from Earth..." Ashtin frowned. "They aren't as technologically advanced as us."

"Their level of advancement is only one fact," Carys said. "There are always things we can learn from others that don't involve technology. The Terrans appear to be smart and resourceful."

"That describes the ones who worked with the Eon," Ashtin said, "but I've read more about the planet Earth. There are a discordant number of countries, all with different creeds, and sometimes, they fight amongst themselves."

Carys raised a brow. "There can be much to learn from differences, as well, Ashtin."

Sten grunted.

Ashtin's comms implant chimed in his ear. He touched his ear. "Go ahead."

"Knightmaster, the ship from Earth is in orbit," a comms officer said.

Across from him, Knightqueen Carys smiled. She'd clearly received the same message.

"The Terran delegation will take a shuttle to the surface shortly," the comms officer continued.

"Thank you," Ashtin said. "Escort them to the castle."

Carys pressed her hands together. "Excellent. Let's go and prepare to greet our guests."

Ashtin fell into step with Sten behind the queen. They traded a look.

It was obvious neither was as excited as their queen. Ashtin couldn't help but feel something was coming. And he had no idea if that *something* was good or bad.

CHAPTER TWO

W*ow.*
As the sleek transport slowed to a stop in front of the Castle Aravena, Kennedy just stared in awe. The entire city was gorgeous, but the castle was breathtaking.

As she stepped out, she half-listened to Douglas and Eve talking. A glance at Davion showed the warrior scanning for threats, not admiring the architecture.

Of course, he'd been here before, and the Eon Empire also had its own stunning architecture, so this wouldn't dazzle him.

But Kennedy wanted to soak up every detail.

The Oronis castle was exactly what she'd pictured a futuristic castle to look like. Blue-and-white spires rose into the air, and the main part of the building had blue windows that gleamed in the sunlight.

It was extraordinary.

She turned and sucked in a breath. The city was

gorgeous, too. There were several other, huge spires—but none as tall as the castle. The rest of the city was spread out below them, with lots of gleaming-white and elegant bridges. And a freaking purple river.

Fancy transports zoomed over the bridge closest to the castle. There were several transports in the air, as well. Overhead, the faded outlines of two huge moons sat in the sky, along with fluffy, white clouds.

"Mom, Dad, I hope you're seeing me right now," she whispered. "This is the adventure of a lifetime." Beep chirped near her ear, and she patted the small drone. "I know, Beep. It's amazing."

Two palace officials stepped out of the grand doorway and greeted them with nods. They wore pure-white jumpsuits.

"Welcome to Castle Aravena," a woman said. "Please come this way. Knightqueen Carys is waiting for you."

"Simply amazing," Claudine murmured, her voice tinged with her French accent. "*Incroyable.*"

Their small group followed the Oronis pair inside. Eve and Davion had left baby Kane on the ship with a carer. Davion took his wife's hand, and Douglas and his wife followed behind. Kennedy brought up the rear.

"Beep, lay low," she murmured.

The small drone gave a low, sad-sounding beep, then slid into a small holster on her belt.

The inside of the castle was just as impressive as the outside, with a white-stone floor and high ceilings. They were led to a glass-walled elevator that whisked them upward, giving them excellent views of the green terraces at the base of the castle. Kennedy looked out at the city again. Lots of greenery was incorporated into many of the buildings. One tall building nearby had what looked like a core of vegetation twisting up at the center of it.

The elevator doors opened.

One of the palace staff members waved a hand for them to go ahead. "Please enter the Grand Hall. The knightqueen is waiting there."

"Thanks." Eve smiled and tugged on Davion's hand. "Come on. This place is so amazing. I want to see more."

"It is impressive," Douglas agreed.

Kennedy was too busy studying what looked like vertical strips of blue crystal set in the walls. Damn, she wanted to touch it and ask a hundred questions.

She studied the huge arched doorway ahead, flanked by a man and a woman.

Then she sucked in a breath.

Knights.

The pair stood to attention, both wearing all-black uniforms. Fitted suits of a supple fabric, and three-quarter-length cloaks.

Their faces were blank, and they stared ahead. As the little group neared, the two knights clicked their heels together and straightened.

"The knightqueen welcomes you." The male guard gestured into the Grand Hall.

Kennedy moved under the arched doorway, then barely stifled a gasp.

The hall was massive, and in here, it was mostly black stone that shone like obsidian, shot through with veins of white and gold. The ceiling soared overhead, and was covered in an intricate web that was threaded with white vines covered in gold flowers. Light filtered down through it, shafts of light hitting the floor.

She looked toward the end of the hall and the air contracted in her chest.

The three people stood waiting for them, even more impressive than the architecture.

She noticed the knightqueen first. The blonde woman stood in front of a magnificent, black throne, carved from dark rock. She was flanked by two men. One was a big bruiser, and Kennedy knew instantly that the man was the queen's bodyguard. He had that watchful alertness she's seen on personal protective specialists. He also had a rugged, scarred face.

Yep, she did not want to be on that man's bad side.

"*Ooh la la,*" Claudine murmured. "The Oronis make their men *very* well." She caught Kennedy's gaze and winked. "A young, single woman like you should take advantage of that."

Stifling a laugh, Kennedy turned her head to look at the other man.

Her skin prickled, and her chest felt tight. He wasn't looking at her, so she took a moment to take in every inch of him.

If she had to pick a man to be a knight, it would be this one. He stood tall and straight, his hands resting at his sides. He wore all black—fitted pants, a doublet that had a high neckline, and a three-quarter cloak like the knights outside.

He was also the most handsome man she'd ever seen. And she'd seen some handsome guys in her time. His face looked carved from stone, with high cheekbones, a strong jaw, sharp blade of a nose. His mouth was unsmiling, and a focused intensity radiated off him. His hair was thick, and pitch-black in color.

She wondered what color his eyes were, and even more, what he looked like when he was fighting.

Her pulse did a hot, little dance.

Then he turned his head, and his gaze clashed with hers.

Kennedy didn't move, but she felt the jolt in her body.

Breathe, Kennedy.

The intensity of his electric-blue stare made her stomach knot and the hairs on the back of her neck rise. His eyes were a deep blue and covered in a web of cracks.

There was a coolness about him, but she wondered if there was heat there, as well.

Correct that, she knew he had heat, and that he controlled it ruthlessly.

His gaze dropped to her uniform, then back up. She got the distinct impression he wasn't happy they were here.

She knew the Oronis weren't xenophobic, but the knights were protective as hell. A part of her wanted to look away, but she refused to be intimidated. She held his stare.

One of his dark eyebrows lifted. A dare, a challenge.

Kennedy's stubbornness rose up. Her aunt was

always telling her that she was as stubborn as a rock. She lifted one of her brows.

She was sure she saw his lips quirk.

"—Sub-Captain Kennedy Black, our Space Corps liaison."

Kennedy realized Eve was talking, and making introductions.

Knightqueen Carys inclined her head. "Welcome. And this is my head knightguard, Sten Carahan, and this is Knightmaster Ashtin Caydor, head of my Knightforce."

Ashtin. The name suited him. Cool, solid, a little haughty.

"Ashtin, why don't you give Sub-Captain Black a tour of the castle?" the knightqueen said. "I'm sure she'd like to be reassured that her charges will be safe during their stay."

Kennedy stiffened. She felt torn. A part of her would sell her soul for a tour, but another part of her was warning her not to tangle with Knightmaster Ashtin.

"IT'S a pleasure to meet you, Sub-Captain Black. It's also my pleasure to give you a tour." Ashtin kept his tone even, pleasant, but he wasn't sure he agreed with the knightqueen's desire to show off the castle's defenses to someone he wasn't sure they could trust yet.

He heard a small sound. Had the sub-captain snorted?

He met her gaze. It was guileless.

His attention scattered as he took in the interesting pale gray color of her eyes.

"Why thank you, Knightmaster. It's much appreciated."

He didn't trust that overly polite tone one bit. He waved a hand, and she moved forward. His gaze dropped. She moved well, and was clearly fit and athletic. He knew a fellow fighter when he saw one.

He dragged his gaze off her.

He never allowed himself to get distracted from his work, his duty. Especially by a woman.

"You work on a Space Corps ship?" he asked.

"Sometimes. I work in the Exploration Division." A smile curled her lips. "I'm a xenoanthropologist. Now that we're working closely with the Eon, we're planning to explore more, and meet new species."

Ashtin made a sound.

She turned. "You aren't convinced?"

"I don't know you or your planet well enough, Sub-Captain."

"Yet." She shot him a smile. "I bet we'll win you over."

She turned and strode ahead, a bounce in her step.

He stared after her for a beat, then followed, frowning.

As they strode out onto the wide balcony of the Grand Hall, he found himself watching the way her hair swung. It was caught up in a tail at the back of her head, and was a deep, rich brown. The same color as the coats of the thoroughbred *cheron* steeds the Oronis knights of old had once ridden into battle.

She was also small. Oronis men and women were tall, but this human wouldn't even reach his shoulder.

She paused at the railing. "You have a beautiful and fascinating city."

He heard amazement and excitement in her voice. His gaze sliced her way. Her tone was almost reverent.

His gaze narrowed. She wasn't looking at his city in an exploitive way. He didn't think she was looking for a way to take it and use it. She just...liked it.

Huge, gray eyes, sparkling with intelligence, met his. "You don't want us here."

Ah, to the point. A part of him admired that. "It isn't personal, Sub-Captain. Like I said, I don't know your planet or your people well enough. I don't believe in taking risks with security."

She smiled, and for some reason, he couldn't look away from her lips.

She nodded. "I get that. I wouldn't want you on Earth studying all our defenses and weaknesses, either."

He stiffened. "We are an honorable people. Service, fealty, protecting those weaker than us is a part of our beliefs, our creed."

"But I don't know that yet." She started down a set of curved steps, then looked back over her shoulder. "I don't know or trust you. Yet."

"The Eon can vouch for us." He followed her, vaguely insulted and irritated. He was supposed to be expressing his concern about her and her people, not the other way around.

"They can vouch for us, too."

Ashtin scowled.

"Besides, you're more technologically advanced than us," she continued. "And you knights are fierce fighters, I hear."

He made a sound. "And from my research, Earth is a chaotic meld of discordant beliefs. You even sometimes war among yourselves. I'm not sure that's trustworthy."

"There are people on Earth who aren't trustworthy, just as I'm sure there are people in this city who aren't trustworthy." She waved an arm at Aravena. "But as a whole, Earth is a planet of people who value freedom. To live life as we choose, without causing harm to others." She paused, drew in a deep breath, then tipped her face to the sun. She looked up at the castle. "It's really beautiful here."

Watching her, he felt annoyance. Mostly because he felt his body reacting to her.

She shot him a look. "I guess trust is earned, Knight-master Ashtin, and that takes more than a day."

They fell into step, walking along one of the castle's main defensive walls.

Suddenly, there was a flurry of beeps, and a small metallic ball whirled up and around Kennedy's head.

Tensing, Ashtin's hand shot out and he grabbed the device.

It whirred against his palm and let out a long beep.

"It's fine." Kennedy whirled and gripped his wrist. "He's mine."

He forgot all about the device. All he could feel was the sensation of her skin on his. Startled, her gaze locked on his.

They stared at each other. What the *gul* was going on here?

Then she pried the ball out of his hand. The drone buzzed around her head like an angry bug.

"It's okay," she said. "You're fine, Beep."

"It's a machine," Ashtin said.

"Yes. His name is Beep."

"He?"

Her chin lifted. "Yes. He's harmless."

There were advanced scanners throughout the palace to detect any dangerous weapons or substances, so he knew the small drone was safe.

She nudged the ball. "Go and explore the gardens. Stay out of trouble."

The drone hovered, seeming to stare balefully at Ashtin for a second, before it sailed over the railing and disappeared.

"Do all Space Corps personnel have a drone?" he asked.

"No. Beep was part of an experimental program. His siblings have all been decommissioned." Her smile was back. She smiled so readily. "Beep is special." She turned back to face the castle grounds. "How many guards do you have?"

"Enough."

She grinned. "I'm going to make you trust me, Knightmaster. One day, you'll spill all your secrets to me."

"I'm an Oronis knight. That will never happen." But he found himself fighting back the unfamiliar need to smile.

She didn't stay quiet for long. "Are guards and knights different?"

That was a question he was happy and willing to answer. "Yes. Knights have increased training, and apprentice with a knightmaster for years before getting their own title. Guards are regular troops. Well-trained, but not to the same level."

"Ah, knights are your special forces. Got it."

"The knightguards of the queen's special bodyguards are also made up of knights, headed by Knightguard Sten."

"He looked like a man no one wants to piss off."

"He's dedicated to the knightqueen. He's been a part of her protection for years."

Kennedy leaned against the railing. "I promise, we're here to forge an alliance, as we've done with the Eon. We want to learn." She flicked a glance to the castle. "And appreciate a new culture. Both our similarities and our differences."

He grunted.

"So skeptical," she said.

"I was born skeptical."

"My aunt says I was born stubborn."

Their gazes met and Ashtin felt a strange zing. Before he could process it, the comm channel on his implant chimed. He touched his ear. "Go ahead."

"Knightmaster, the perimeter sensors went off." There was heavy tension in the comm officer's voice. "Something breached the wall."

Ashtin stiffened. "What?"

"We have no visual, sir. We're not sure what it is. It appears blurred on the security feed."

Ashtin cursed, scanning the gardens below.

Kennedy stepped up beside him, looking down, as well. "What's happening?"

"Go back inside," he ordered.

"No," she said. "I can help."

He gritted his teeth. "Sub-Captain, something just breached the castle perimeter—"

"Call me Kennedy." Then she stiffened and pointed. "Look."

In the garden below, he spotted a patch of blurriness under the branches of a nearby *sinata*.

Coolness moved through him. An enemy thought they could infiltrate the planet, the city, the castle grounds.

Not on his watch.

With a single thought, his combat implants flared to life, energy running through him. His black armor, made from a nanotech substance, flowed from the implants embedded along his spine.

He heard Kennedy gasp.

The armor moved around his body, snapping into place on his chest. He glanced at her, their gazes locking, before his black visor slid over his face.

"Stay back." Ashtin gripped the railing, then jumped on to it for a second, before leaping into the air.

He sailed out, then dropped down to the garden below. His armor compensated, a small blast of energy letting him land easily with a bend of his knees.

Where are you? He scanned for the intruder, the

heads-up display in his visor filled with information as he searched for the enemy. He couldn't see the blurred presence anywhere.

But he would find them.

He lifted his palms. Energy built, pulling from his veins. It grew into a bright-blue ball, crackling between his palms.

Time to hunt.

CHAPTER THREE

K ennedy stared at Ashtin in amazement.

He moved well—fast and lethal. She watched him sail through the air, that dangerous black armor making him look like a deadly weapon. He seemed to slow a little before he reached the ground, and Kennedy was desperate to know how that kickass armor worked.

She watched him land: powerful, strong, and ready to fight.

Scanning the ground, she couldn't see that blurred attacker now. He had to be hiding in the garden shrubbery.

She figured Ashtin couldn't spot him, either, as he started striding through the garden, searching. Then, a crackle of energy filled the air. Blue electricity formed between Ashtin's palms.

Oh. She took the stairs two at a time. She wanted to be close enough to watch, and to help.

He might be a lethal space knight, but she sucked at being a damsel, or standing still.

She reached the garden and wished she had a weapon. A nearby tree had some decent-sized branches. She gripped one, and heaved, snapping it off.

Ashtin was still crossing the garden like a dark predator.

Kennedy moved stealthily in his direction. She shifted through the bushes, some of them taller than she was. Sunlight dappled her skin. She listened carefully, could hear birds tweeting happily.

Where are you?

The birdsong cut off. She heard a snap of a twig and turned slowly. Then she caught a blur of movement.

She edged through a bush. *Come out, come out, wherever you are.*

She turned, and saw a blurred figure step into the sunlight.

There.

Kennedy ran, leaped onto a low, stone wall, then jumped off it. She lifted her branch. She whacked it down on the attacker, hard.

The being grunted, and the intruder's fancy camouflage shimmered. She caught the vague impression of a misshapen outline.

"Ashtin!" she yelled.

The intruder launched forward and rammed into her. The force of the blow lifted her off her feet.

Shit.

She hit the ground on her side, teeth clicking together. Her temple and cheek hit a rock, and the pain made her wince. She rolled onto her back and looked up.

The blurred figure loomed above her, lifting a rock from the ground. It looked like it was levitating.

Oh, hell. She pulled her legs up, ready to kick.

A large, black shadow leaped over her. Ashtin threw a blue ball of energy, and it hit the attacker in the chest. The thing roared, and for a second, part of its camouflage failed.

Kennedy saw an ugly face covered in scales and ridges, a flat nose, and wide-set eyes. The alien had sharp, narrow teeth in its wide mouth. Its body was warped, and it had a hunchback covered in more green scales.

Ashtin whirled. Blue energy in the shape of blades cut out of his forearms. They cut through the air and into the attacker. They embedded deep, and the reptilian creature fell, tumbling back into a garden bed.

The thing wasn't dead. She could see it moving and struggling. Ashtin advanced.

As she scrambled up, she saw the alien lift a weapon and fire.

Ashtin dived to the left, rolling agilely. A blast of green laser hit a tree, and the branches caught fire.

Fuck.

Heart pounding, Kennedy crawled, staying low. The alien tracked Ashtin as the knight ran, firing its deadly weapon.

No, you don't. Kennedy grabbed a sharp-ended stick off the ground. She didn't stop to think. She scrambled up and ran at the attacker.

He heard her at the last second, but she jumped and rammed the stick into one of his large eyes.

His scream was hoarse and raspy, and he dropped his weapon.

Ashtin was there a second later.

More blue blades sliced out of his forearms, and cut into the attacker, pinning him to the dirt.

The alien's screams cut off. His camouflage dropped and his body slumped.

Kennedy sat on the ground, her chest heaving. She looked up. Ashtin was staring at her, like he'd never seen her before.

She stared back. "What?"

"You didn't follow orders." He strode toward her. "I said to stay back."

"Well, you should get used to that. I do what I think is right." She touched her temple and cheek. They were stinging.

Ashtin knelt in front of her, his three-quarter coat flaring on the grass behind him. She stilled. He was so close. God, his eyes were remarkable. They were a rich blue and filled with cracks, that made her think of shattered ice.

And that damn jawline and high cheekbones. She wanted to bite him.

What was wrong with her?

"I thought you were a xenoanthropologist," he said.

"I am."

"You fight well."

"I train. Everyone in Space Corps does." She lifted a shoulder. "And I am voraciously curious and love learning new things. I've taken several advanced combat classes."

He reached out. She watched armor retract from his hand and up his arm, leaving a long-fingered hand covered in bronze skin.

He touched her cheek. "You're bleeding."

"It's just a small scrape." Her belly clenched. His fingers were warm, and she felt that touch deep inside her.

Of course, she was attracted to him. He was like a fantasy pulled from every woman's head, not to mention he fought well, moved well. And that cool, outer shell... It tempted a woman to crack it and find the heat inside.

Get a grip on it, Kennedy.

He held out a hand and she took it, clenching her teeth at the sensation. He was watching her like a hawk as he helped her up.

Kennedy glanced down at the...thing on the ground. "That is ugly."

"Yes, it is." His voice was as sharp as a honed blade.

The thing looked like an ogre. Like it had just stepped out of some dark fairytale.

"What is it?" she asked.

"It is a *dirlox*. A reptilian alien species from beyond our borders. You don't see them often. They have low intelligence, but are very aggressive." He crouched, and touched the pack attached to the dirlox's chest.

"And that?"

"It looks like some sort of generator."

"For the camouflage," she said. "Do they all have stealth camouflage like this one?"

Those cracked blue eyes met hers. "No." He rose in a

fluid move. "I do know they're often used by the Gek'Dragar."

She didn't know the word. The dark edge to his voice had her fighting back a shiver. "Gek'Dragar?"

"Our enemy."

The sound of shouts and running footsteps caught Kennedy's ear. A group of knights and guards were jogging toward them.

"Looks like the cavalry is here," she said.

Ashtin met her gaze again. "Thank you for the assistance, Kennedy."

She felt a flush of heat, and hoped it didn't show on her face.

OKAY, it was official, Kennedy was going to move into this shower and live in it.

She tilted her head under the running water. The bathroom adjoined the bedroom she'd been assigned in the castle. The walls were made of the same black stone as the Great Hall, and crisscrossed with veins of gold and white that glowed in the light. The huge rain showerhead covered most of the top of the shower, and the water itself had a silky feel that left her skin smooth.

Finally, she made herself get out, grabbed a thin, drying sheet that was super absorbent, then stepped onto the semicircle of rock outside the shower. Blowers started, warm air drying her off as she toweled her hair dry.

The bathroom had a huge, round mirror, and a round

tub made of white stone, and several lush green plants. Smiling, she fingered a shiny, green leaf. It curled almost affectionately around her finger, startling a laugh out of her.

Then she wrapped the drying sheet around her body and turned to the mirror.

She had a graze on her temple and a cut on her cheek. She touched them. They weren't too bad, but she'd need a little extra makeup magic to hide it for the ball in a few hours.

She wondered about the *dirlox* from the day before.

What was its mission? Why did it sneak onto the castle grounds? She had drawn a sketch of it and taken notes about the encounter on her tablet.

She was sure Ashtin and the knights had things under control.

Ashtin.

Goose bumps prickled over her skin. She'd dreamed of him last night. Watching him fight, seeing him walk toward her, his gaze intense.

Even now, she shivered.

She blew out a breath. She hadn't seen him since the incident in the garden yesterday. Last night, her group had been given a meal with the knightqueen on a huge terrace. The night view of the city of Aravena was just as stunning as during the day.

Kennedy had then stayed up way too late recording all her initial observations of Aravena and the Oronis. Beep had supplied her with lots of images to add to her records.

Then today, she, Eve, and Claudine had toured some

of the public areas of the castle. The staff had all been busy, decorating and preparing for the ball.

She'd also seen lots of ground shuttles arriving and disgorging elegantly dressed guests. Despite her disinterest in needing to primp, she was excited to see the ball. She absolutely loved the idea of seeing the other species and cultures.

And are you excited to see Knightmaster Ashtin again?

She cleared her throat. Well, she did want to speak to him again. She wanted to know more about the intruder. That was her story, and she was sticking to it.

She stepped out of the bathroom and jerked to a halt.

Her bedroom was no longer empty. Eve was playing with baby Kane on the rug. The cute little boy could sit up, and it looked like he was thinking about crawling. He had dark hair like Eve, and his father's blue-black eyes. Kane turned his head and gave her a grin.

Claudine was lounging on Kennedy's bed.

Kennedy hitched up her drying sheet. "Are you guys lost?"

Eve grinned, and held out the toy Kennedy had given to her son. The little boy latched onto it, shaking it wildly. "We brought you your dress." Eve nodded.

Kennedy glanced at the black dress laid out on the bed beside Claudine.

"It is *superbe*," Claudine drawled. "It will look stunning on you." The woman smiled. "All the dresses tonight are black or white. Only the knightqueen will wear gold. I cannot wait. I hear the ball will be simply beautiful. I am wearing white."

"My dress is black, too," Eve said.

The dress on the bed looked sparkly, and Kennedy would've preferred it to be plainer, but at least it wasn't poofy. She could hopefully stay under the radar, and just observe the ball.

"Any word on the intruder from yesterday?" Kennedy asked.

Eve shook her head. "I know Davion talked with Ashtin. They've increased security."

"Do you know who the Gek'Dragar are?" She'd been searching her files for any reference to the species, but hadn't found anything.

Eve helped Kane scoot closer, then he pulled himself up, clinging to her. "Davion's heard of them. Apparently, they're bad news. Some humanoid reptilian species that are enemies of the Oronis. The two species had huge wars hundreds of years ago. Terrible losses on both sides, but the Oronis fought them off. They haven't been seen for centuries."

"It was one of these Gek'Dragar that snuck into the castle garden?" Claudine sat up, frowning.

"No," Kennedy said. "It was something called a *dirlox*, but apparently, they're linked to the Gek'Dragar. Knightmaster Ashtin didn't look happy about it."

Eve lifted Kane into her arms and stood. "I'm sure everything will be fine. There's a huge security presence at the castle, and across the city. And if anything gets inside, Ashtin and the knights will stop it. You should see them fight."

"I saw him yesterday."

Eve met Kennedy's gaze, and her lips quirked. "They're something else, aren't they?"

Ashtin sure was something.

She wanted to know more about his armor and how it formed. She knew the Eon could form armor and weapons, but they had a bond with a small symbiont alien that allowed them to manipulate energy. Ashtin's abilities looked different.

Kennedy felt that familiar hum of curiosity.

Kane grabbed a handful of his mother's hair and yanked. Eve winced. "Right, I need to go and feed my little man, then get ready for this ball."

Claudine paused by Kennedy. "Your grazes will need hiding."

Kennedy fingered her cheek. "It'll be fine. I can do my makeup."

"Make it dramatic. This isn't a dinner party, it's a ball." Claudine waved a hand. "Smoky eyes, Kennedy, or I'll put makeup on you myself."

"Fine. Fine."

"*Bien. Au revoir.*"

Kennedy saw them out, then moved to study the dress. As she got closer, she squinted.

Oh, hell. It had a halter top, with a strip of fabric that would wrap around her neck like a choker, but the neckline in the center dipped all the way to her waist. And the dress had no back.

She fingered the fabric. She wouldn't be able to wear a bra. She frowned. When she found out who'd picked this, she'd give them a piece of her mind.

Heading back to the bathroom, she got to work on her

makeup. Since her shoulders, back, and arms would be bare, she rubbed on a cream that gave her a golden glow.

Beep appeared, darting around her.

"Have you been exploring?"

A quick beep.

"I hope you got lots of images for me."

Another beep. Then he bumped her shoulder.

"No, you can't come, buddy. Not tonight."

Her drone gave a slow, sad beep. Then it nudged her scraped temple.

"It's okay. It's nothing."

She did her best to cover the scratches with makeup, then did some smoky eyes. She was a little scared of letting Claudine near her with makeup.

Kennedy kept her hair simple. She put some styling lotion on it, slicked it back, and parted it down the middle.

In just black panties and heels that had an ankle strap —and thankfully weren't too high—she headed back to the bed. Next, she lifted a small combat knife and sheath out of her bag.

No one would see it strapped to her thigh under her dress.

Finally, she pulled on the dress.

Then she turned to the mirror on the wall.

Her mouth dropped open, and she groaned.

Maybe she wouldn't fade into the background. She prayed everyone else had much more eye-catching dresses than she did.

The dress clung to her body, and the fabric shimmered in the light. She realized now that there were several patches that were see-through, showing off her legs. The low neckline displayed plenty of skin. Thank God her boobs weren't too big, or she'd be in trouble.

She sucked in a deep breath. She was sure that the Oronis citizens would have super-fancy outfits. This would be nothing.

There was a knock on the door. After a deep breath, she headed over. Her group were on time to collect her.

As soon as she opened the door, Eve whistled. "Kennedy, you are hot."

"*Très belle*." Claudine clapped her hands together.

Both men nodded at her.

"What Eve said," Davion agreed. His wife elbowed him. "I'm just stating a fact." Then he yanked his wife in close. "You're still the hottest woman I know."

Eve melted against her mate.

The couple looked gorgeous. Eve's black dress with a full skirt that had an asymmetrical hem that was higher in the front, showing off her toned legs. Claudine's dress was white, in a mermaid style, and an off-the-shoulder neckline, with a dramatic ruffle. Her blonde hair was loose. Douglas was in a suit, while Davion wore an Eon outfit that molded to his muscular body, and was sleeveless.

"Well, let's get this over with." Kennedy closed the door before Beep could escape.

"This is a ball, Kennedy," Claudine said. "You're supposed to have fun. Dance, flirt with a handsome man."

Kennedy just grunted. As they approached the Grand Hall, a small crowd was waiting to enter.

The outfits were amazing. The black-and-white color scheme was eye-catching, and most of the women's dresses were bold, with structural elements that looked like something off a runway, or an art show. The men all wore black.

The men got off easy for formal events, it seemed, whatever planet you were on.

Finally, their group entered the Hall.

"Oh, *magnifique*," Claudine murmured.

"Wow," Eve echoed.

Kennedy just stared, her hands itching for a camera. The hall looked like some fantasy-film setting. The vines overhead glowed, and were loaded with flowers. The long, tall windows of blue glass overlooked the city. Music was playing.

Her heart pounded. *This* was why she wanted to explore space. To see new things. To see things like *this*.

A part of her understood her parents' need to always leave and explore.

The music changed, more elegant strings coming into play. She looked over and saw an elegant Oronis woman step up on a small stage. Her dress was a brilliant silver-white, with an ethereal, floaty skirt and a strapless bodice that clung to her slender frame. Her black hair was piled up on top of her head.

The woman closed her eyes, lifted her hands, and started to sing.

Kennedy gasped. She didn't understand the words, but the woman's voice was pure and haunting. The others in Kennedy's group turned to look at the singer.

The music swelled and so did the woman's beautiful

voice, ringing across the Hall. Kennedy had no idea what the woman was singing about, but emotions swelled inside her and her throat tightened. She thought of love and loss, hopes and dreams. It was like the song reached inside Kennedy's chest and hit her in the heart.

"She's incredible," Eve murmured.

She sure was. Then the back of Kennedy's neck prickled, and she turned.

And looked directly into the gaze of Knightmaster Ashtin.

He was standing with the knightqueen. He wore all black again—another set of fitted black pants, a doublet-style shirt edged with gold, and a three-quarter cape that fell off his shoulders.

He looked annoyingly attractive. A low throb pulsed deep in her belly.

Forging an alliance and gaining their trust doesn't involve imagining the knightmaster naked, Kennedy. She swallowed, trying to get her unruly body under control. She was here to work, and couldn't afford to screw anything up.

She gave him a crisp nod and turned away.

But Kennedy could still feel his gaze boring into her.

CHAPTER FOUR

Ashtin scanned the Grand Hall, watching more and more guests appear.

They were mostly Oronis, all important people of Aravena and its surrounds. The guests from the other species stood out. The blue-skinned Phideans, and the rotund Borusians.

He clasped his hands behind his back, still searching for one brown-haired woman.

As one of the evening's singers started, Sten appeared beside him. The man's gaze was locked on the knightqueen as she greeted guests. She looked stunning in her dark-gold dress and black crown. Her white-blonde hair was up in a complicated twist.

"I can't trace how the *dirlox* got onto the planet." Sten sounded very unhappy about the thought.

Ashtin made a sound. "It must have been smuggled in."

"By who?"

"One of the guests." Ashtin's muscles tightened. "Ultimately, the Gek'Dragar have to be responsible."

Sten grunted. "No one wants war again, but if they try to touch the queen, I'll slaughter them all."

Ashtin knew the man meant every word.

Sten was right. No one wanted war, but the Oronis knights had grown stronger over the centuries. They were now heavily enhanced. They had combat implants, not to mention the *oralite*—a small, powerful nano-implant embedded at the base of the neck that melded with a knight's brainstem. and powered their armor and implants. It allowed them to utilize pure power.

Pure energy.

They could generate energy balls, create an energy blade, or throw up a shield.

It made them deadly.

The conflict with the Gek'Dragar had forced the Oronis to try more lethal enhancements. It had led them to implanting the first *oralite* in a knight. His hand flexed. He still remembered having his own implanted at the age of thirteen. "They will face the full power of the Oronis knights if they attack."

Sten nodded.

Then Ashtin sensed her. Like a prickling caress along his skin.

He turned his head and saw Kennedy Black. He sucked in a sharp breath.

The dress clung to her fit body, and highlighted the curve of her hips. It was cut low, and showed hints of her breasts. He swallowed. Her hair was slicked back, showcasing her features. They weren't fine or delicate like most Oronis women's, they were bolder, stronger.

She met his gaze, and didn't look away. The lights shimmered off the glossy, black filaments in her dress.

Its simplicity made her stand out.

Then she nodded and turned away.

"Ashtin? Ashtin?"

He barely controlled his jerk. Sten was talking to him. "Sorry. What did you say?"

Sten glanced between Ashtin and Kennedy, then frowned. "Are you...distracted? By a woman?"

"I don't get distracted," Ashtin clipped.

He wouldn't let the Space Corps sub-captain distract him. But he couldn't take his gaze off her.

Suddenly, a tall, regal couple entered the room. Kennedy and her group hurried over to them with smiles.

The man was pure Eon warrior—tall and broad, with a sense of authority. The woman at his side was tall as well, with a long body, and dark hair.

Ashtin recognized the King and Queen of the Eon Empire.

He watched Kennedy embrace Queen Alea. The woman was a former Space Corps officer, herself.

"Oh good, Gayel is here." Carys joined Sten and Ashtin. "He looks so incredibly happy with his mate."

The king slid an arm around his wife, who wore a white, strapless dress.

Ashtin glanced at Carys. He thought he detected a touch of envy in her voice.

"Now, I know you two are here plotting more security measures and agonizing over the *dirlox*."

Ashtin looked at Sten. The knightguard was blank faced.

"You've tripled security," Carys said. "So now I want you to have fun."

Sten crossed his brawny arms.

Carys got a stubborn look on her face. The light glinted off her intricate gold earrings. "I mean it, Thorsten. You'll have fun."

Ashtin hid a smile. There was no way Sten was having or would have anything remotely like fun with so many people around the queen.

"That's an order, Knightguard," Carys said. "Ashtin, show him how it's done."

Ashtin stiffened. "Your Highness—"

"Don't you start with that *Your Highness* business. Dance." She waved a hand at the empty dance floor. The musicians were playing delicate Oronis music that was mostly strings and bells.

"My queen—"

"Go and ask Sub-Captain Black to dance." Carys smiled, looking at him expectantly.

By the coward's bones. With a small bow, he strode across the ballroom.

As he approached, Kennedy's head whipped up. She watched him warily.

"Knightmaster Ashtin." King Gayel smiled, and held out an arm.

"King Gayel." They pressed their forearms together in a warrior's clasp. "Welcome to Oron." He looked over at the Eon queen. "Queen Alea."

"We don't need the queen bit." The woman smiled. "Alea is fine."

Ashtin nodded and looked at Kennedy. "Sub-Captain, I'd like to show you some Oronis dance steps."

Her gray eyes popped wide. "Dance? Oh, I—"

The ambassador's wife nudged her forward, and she almost collided with him. He grabbed her elbow.

"She'd love to," the blonde woman drawled, beaming.

Ashtin led a stiff Kennedy to the dance floor, and nodded at the musicians. He wrapped his arms around her. "Place your arms around my neck."

She reluctantly obeyed. As the music started, she swallowed. "I'm not a good dancer, and I don't know the steps."

"Just follow my lead. You told me you like to learn new things."

She huffed. "Not with hundreds of people watching."

"You can fight, and dancing is a lot like fighting. Just give yourself over to the movements. Commit, don't be hesitant."

He moved, and she followed. They took a few missteps, but she caught on quickly. Soon, they were moving smoothly across the floor, in perfect sync.

She felt so good in his arms, her body brushing against his. She was wearing a scent unlike anything on Oron—sweet, spicy. It was driving him crazy.

They whirled around the dance floor.

"The music is fascinating. That stringed instrument looks difficult to use." She paused, then murmured, "people are staring at us."

"I rarely dance, so they're wondering who you are. The woman who tempted the knightmaster."

Her gaze flicked to his. "Why did you ask me?"

"My queen ordered me to."

He thought he saw a flash of disappointment, but she quickly looked away.

"Of course. And you always obey orders."

He leaned down, his voice a low whisper. "And because I couldn't drag my gaze off you."

She looked back up quickly, her eyes wide.

Ashtin felt a flush of annoyance. "I don't want to feel this pull. I never have before."

"Well, the feeling is mutual. And I don't like it either." Her fingers dug into his shoulders.

Other dancers joined in, but Ashtin barely noticed.

She felt this attraction, too. He pulled her closer, and her body melted against his.

He swallowed a groan. She was perfection. Strong but feminine. Smart. A little defiant.

Kennedy looked up and he saw heat in her gaze.

The music swelled around them. He was supposed to be focused on the ball, on security, not how her hips felt under his hands. Or how gray her eyes were.

On the next circle of the dance floor, he whisked her out the open doors onto the balcony.

THE COOL AIR hit her heated skin.

Ashtin was holding Kennedy's hand tightly, and he

pulled her toward the end of the balcony. It was drenched in shadows.

The city spread out beneath them, and her breath caught. She stared at the beautiful glitter of white lights, and the purple glow of the river.

She was so aware of the man beside her—his big, hard body, his cool, controlled presence. She couldn't stop thinking about the way he'd held her. The way he'd moved against her while they'd danced.

She was so aware of him it almost hurt.

He spun her and pressed her against the stone wall of the castle.

"I can't stop thinking about you," he murmured.

He definitely didn't sound happy about it.

"I'm not doing anything," she said.

"I know." His blue eyes glittered. "Apparently, you just have to breathe." He leaned closer, breathed deeply. "You smell so good."

"It's my perfume. Honeysuckle. It's a plant on Earth."

"I am an Oronis knight. I am in full control at all times."

"Are you trying to convince me or yourself?" She pressed her hands to his chest, feeling the hard thump of his heart. Her own was racing. "I keep thinking about the way you fought the *dirlox.*"

His gaze bored into hers. "And I keep thinking of your courage. The way you attacked it with no weapon except a stick."

"I don't need a weapon to be dangerous."

"Oh, I know."

"I took a training course on improvising and using anything in reach as a weapon."

He traced a finger down her bare arm.

"I'm good at improvising." Damn, she was rambling. She shivered, feeling his touch everywhere. She throbbed between her legs.

Suddenly, she didn't hear the music and conversation from inside anymore. The only thing in her ears was the rapid thump of her heartbeat. The only thing she could see was the man staring down at her. And the only thing she could feel was the urgent, fierce need inside her.

Her hands curled in his black shirt. She heard him mutter a curse, then she pulled his head down.

Their lips clashed, and Kennedy finally got a taste of Knightmaster Ashtin.

God.

Holy freaking hell.

His mouth took hers, tongue stroking deep. He kissed even better than she'd imagined.

She pressed into him, moaning. He made a sound, palms pressing to the stone either side of her head.

Their tongues tangled, and the taste of him was delicious. She slid her arms around his neck, her fingers toying with his thick, black hair.

Kennedy suddenly never wanted to do anything else except kiss this man. She'd happily stay right here, kissing him, for the rest of her life.

Then he lifted his head, and she made a sound of protest.

He stared at her, his hands now gripping her hips, then his mouth crashed back down on hers.

Kennedy needed more. She needed to get closer. She gripped the skirt of her dress, then jumped up, wrapping her legs around his hips.

He growled into her mouth, his hands sliding under her ass. He pressed her into the wall, his tongue delving into her mouth, his hips pressing between her legs. She ground against the sizable erection she felt.

Oh boy, she was in so much trouble.

"*Kennedy*." His voice was a rasp, his mouth nipping at her neck.

"Ashtin," she breathed.

"Tell me to stop."

"Hell, no."

Then his mouth was on hers again.

At that moment, all the lights in the castle went off, plunging them into darkness.

Ashtin stiffened.

Frowning, Kennedy stared over his shoulder. *What the hell?* She watched as the lights of the city winked out. Like a dark wave moving away from the castle, washing out over Aravena.

"Ashtin?"

He set her down and they turned. They watched the darkness envelop the capital of Oron.

"What's going on?" she asked.

"The power's out." His voice was grim. "We have several contingencies to avoid a situation like this."

She looked up at him. He was just a shadow in the darkness. "Which means?"

"Which means this is no accident."

Her muscles tightened. "I need to find the ambassador and—"

Suddenly, all the windows of the Grand Hall blew out.

There was a roar of noise, and crashing glass, then a heavy weight was driving her to the stone floor. Ashtin covered her, wrapping his larger body around her.

Screams broke out inside.

"Up," she barked. She had to get to her group. "We need to get inside."

"When it's safe."

"Ashtin! We need to get in there."

He hesitated.

"I'm a sub-captain. I don't need protecting."

He rose and hauled her up. Then something above caught her gaze.

Something was climbing over the castle wall. It had a big, strong body, blocking out the stars in the night sky.

Ashtin looked up and tensed.

Hell, she wished she had a weapon. "What is that?" she murmured.

"I can't tell," he answered.

His tense voice said it wasn't anything good.

"Hey!" Kennedy yelled.

Whatever the creature was, it stilled. She could sense it looking at them.

Then it tensed and leaped at them.

Oh, shit.

Ashtin knocked her out of the way. The alien landed on the balcony with a thud, then straightened.

Kennedy stared at the large being. It was just over six

feet tall, with powerful legs and broad shoulders. It was humanoid, except for the long, scaled tail she saw waving behind it.

Moonlight filtered over the alien. It took a step forward and she sucked in a breath. It wore a high-tech suit that gleamed in the silvery light. Its neck and face weren't covered.

Its face was almost regal, with pale gray, scaled skin at the neck that darkened to almost black at the forehead. Two ridges ran along its sharp cheekbones, and four bony horns—two each side—sweeping back from its face. Long, black hair swept down to its shoulders. Deep-green eyes glowed in the dark.

There was a flash of blue light. Ashtin stood, his feet planted, his arms raised, and his gaze locked on the alien. His combat armor was on, and blue energy crackled, growing between his palms.

The alien shifted.

"Stay where you are, Gek'Dragar," Ashtin said, his tone icy.

Gek'Dragar.

This was a Gek'Dragar?

The mortal enemy of the Oronis.

CHAPTER FIVE

G *ek'Dragar*. Ashtin stared at the alien. He'd only seen one once before.

It was strong, with heavy musculature. And a cold gaze as it assessed them.

The screams from inside increased and he saw flashes of blue light.

The knights were fighting back.

Ashtin's muscles tightened. Sten and his knight-guards would protect the queen.

Now, Ashtin had to protect Kennedy.

Of course, she didn't look afraid. She was studying the Gek'Dragar carefully. She looked like she was cataloguing the alien for strengths and weaknesses.

By the coward's bones. With a jolt of certainty, he knew the stubborn woman from Earth wouldn't stay back or run for safety.

"I do not take orders from my enemy," the Gek'-Dragar clipped.

Then it let out a low rumble and threw its arms out

wide. As Ashtin watched, its body started to enlarge, growing taller and wider.

"What the hell?" Kennedy muttered.

Ashtin nudged her back, his jaw tightening. "The *var*."

"The what? What's it doing?"

Ashtin backed up. "Our stories say that the Gek'-Dragar could change on the battlefield into a warrior form. They'd get larger, stronger, more beast-like. They would rampage into battle." He'd always hoped the stories were exaggerated.

"God," she murmured. "Like a berserker rage."

She sounded half horrified, half intrigued.

With a roar, the Gek'Dragar towered over them. Its hands were now tipped with long claws and its tail was covered in spikes. The ridges on his face were heavier, his horns longer.

Then the Gek'Dragar attacked.

It launched its massive body forward, lifting strong arms and huge claws.

Ashtin dodged and tossed up a ball of energy.

The energy ball hit the alien in the center of its chest. It roared—a low, guttural sound. The blue light crackled over him.

The alien dropped to one knee, the stone floor of the balcony cracking under the force of its body.

Ashtin formed a blue blade and threw it. It sailed toward the Gek'Dragar.

The alien rolled, narrowly avoiding losing its head. When it came up, it snatched a blaster weapon off its belt and fired.

The laser hit Ashtin in the gut. His armor absorbed it, but the momentum knocked him back and slammed him into the wall.

"Ashtin!"

He heard Kennedy's shout and his vision wavered. He wasn't injured, but the blow still hurt. He struggled to pull in a breath.

Then he saw her moving.

No. She needed to stay back. He saw her reach under the skirt of her dress.

What was the little fool up to?

She pulled out a sleek blade. She swiveled to face the Gek'Dragar.

The alien rose to its full height, towering over her.

"Come on, asshole," she cried.

"What are you?" The Gek'Dragar's voice was deep and raspy. It cocked its head, its green eyes assessing her. "A small, inferior female."

Ashtin fought to get his body moving. He had to save her.

Kennedy smiled, and there was an edge to it. "Inferior? Inferior? Jeez, even reptilian alien males are dense."

She threw her knife.

It sliced into one of the Gek'Dragar's eyes.

The alien roared. Kennedy leaped and landed a kick to the Gek'Dragar's chest. The alien staggered back, but not far.

"Who's inferior now?" She leaped onto the stone railing, causing Ashtin's heart to lodge in his throat. He pushed forward, fighting back his pain.

Kennedy jumped, and her kick snapped the Gek'-Dragar's head back.

The alien crashed to one knee, but swiped out with his clawed hand. The tips of it shredded the fabric of her dress.

She evaded and rolled across the balcony. The Gek'-Dragar went after her.

Ashtin formed a blade and shot it from his palm. But he was moving so fast it went wild, slicing over the alien's head.

The alien stalked toward Kennedy. She was still crouched, but she caught Ashtin's gaze. His heart was thumping hard as he ran toward her.

Then she winked at him.

Shock rocketed through him.

The Gek'Dragar raised a claw.

Kennedy grabbed a broken shard of stone from where the Gek'Dragar's knees had shattered the floor. She raised the stone and threw it hard.

It crashed into the alien's face, hitting the knife still lodged there. He bellowed.

"Now!" Kennedy yelled.

Ashtin jumped, and mid-air, he formed a long, sword with a blade of pure, blue energy.

He fell on the Gek'Dragar and skewered the blade into the back of the alien's neck.

The Gek'Dragar's shout cut off, and the alien slumped to the floor. A pool of blood grew under the large, motionless body. Then the body shrunk, its armor changing with it, claws dissolving, until it was back to its original size.

Ashtin's blade dissolved. He strode toward Kennedy, his visor sliding back.

She was smiling.

"That was a good fight," she said.

"Your reckless, incautious, foolish—"

She put her hand on her hip and raised a brow. "You're welcome."

The sound of more fighting came from inside.

Her smile disappeared. "We need to help. I need to find my people." She leaned down and yanked her knife out of the Gek'Dragar's eye.

He growled. "Stay behind me."

She snorted. "You already know that isn't happening."

Together, they jogged to the doors. It was so dark in the hall, it was hard to tell what was happening. Ashtin's visor slid back into place, and he switched to night vision.

Chaos.

People were running and screaming.

And fighting.

He saw several Oronis knights fighting the *gul*-vexed Gek'Dragar. All were in their warrior forms.

Where was the knightqueen?

He saw a large warrior holding a sword that glowed lighter blue. Davion swung, taking down a Gek'Dragar. A woman in black scale armor ran beside him, and fired her blaster. *Eve.*

Another couple leaped into the fight, both in Eon armor. Alea carried a purple sword and Gayel threw his arms out. A rush of energy hit a trio of Gek'Dragar.

Suddenly, a low boom echoed through the building.

Kennedy grabbed Ashtin's arm. "What now?"

He spotted a Gek'Dragar with the device on the floor. He was pressing what appeared to be controls. Another low boom, but this time, a burst of green light rippled out of the device like a wave.

When it hit Ashtin, he went blind.

He couldn't see. All the energy drained out of him. He felt his armor melt away.

He crashed to the floor.

"Ashtin! *Ashtin!*"

He managed to pry one eye open. His temporary blindness faded, but everything was blurry. He saw other Oronis knights collapsing across the hall.

No. *No.*

He felt Kennedy's fingers touch his face.

"Ashtin?"

But he couldn't move. He couldn't protect her.

NOISE AND CHAOS echoed around the hall.

But as Kennedy watched Ashtin collapse, like a puppet with its strings cut, pure horror filled her.

The light. The green light had done something to him.

Around the hall, other knights were falling, too.

Leaving them vulnerable. Leaving the Oronis citizens defenseless.

"Eve! Davion!" Kennedy crouched by Ashtin.

The couple raced over, both splattered with blood.

"The Gek'Dragar did something. The Oronis knights are down. We need to protect them."

Davion cursed. He grabbed his mate's arm. "Come on." He turned and bellowed. "Gayel, protect the knights."

Eve shoved a blaster into Kennedy's hand. "Here you go."

"Thanks." She gripped the weapon tightly.

It was still dark inside, and she could only make out moving shadows. She knew that some of them belonged to the attacking Gek'Dragar.

She pushed Ashtin's hair back. "Wake up, Galahad." The perfect nickname for him. *I'm not letting them hurt you.*

She prayed he'd be okay and wake up soon.

The sound of glass crunching under heavy boots, followed by a guttural roar. She saw more aliens leap through the broken windows.

Fierce resolve filled her.

One of the Gek'Dragar spotted Ashtin and stormed over. She saw a guest run out of the alien's way, screaming.

Kennedy straightened. "Back off, asshole."

He towered over her, spiked tail waving steadily behind him like a snake. He made a raspy sound, and she realized he was laughing.

Anger exploded inside her.

She raised her blaster and fired.

The Gek'Dragar jerked. The laser blast ricocheted harmlessly off its armor. She aimed for the face, but he whirled away.

Then he spun back and charged. Adrenaline spiked, and she kept firing.

He slammed into her and knocked her backward into a table of drinks. Glasses flew everywhere, smashing.

Kennedy bounced back up, shaking her head. The alien swiveled, his gaze locking on Ashtin's motionless form.

It reached over its shoulder and pulled out a long sword.

Her stomach locked. *No.* She grabbed a broken glass.

It wasn't much, but it was all she had. She sprinted the distance to the alien and leaped, then jumped onto the Gek'Dragar's broad back.

He made a surprised sound.

"You do *not* get to hurt him." She rammed the glass into the alien's skin at its neck. It roared. The skin was softer there.

She stabbed again and felt a splash of blood. The Gek'Dragar staggered.

Another hit and it toppled, right beside Ashtin. The knightmaster still hadn't moved.

Kennedy stayed on top of the alien, and rammed an elbow into his face. She caught one of his horns on the downward swing, its sharp edge cutting her arm, but she didn't stop. Finally, he stopped moving beneath her.

She climbed off and darted over to Ashtin. She realized his eyes were open, and he was watching her.

"The time for resting is over, Galahad," she said.

He blinked, but didn't move.

"You still can't move?" She ran a hand down his body

and felt his leg twitch. "I think it's wearing off. Hang in there."

Looking up, Kennedy assessed the hall. The King of Eon was fighting two Gek'Dragar, along with Alea. She was just as impressive as her mate.

Several more Oronis guards thundered into the hall, joining the fight. Guests who hadn't made it out safely cowered behind the tables.

Suddenly, a female knight raced into the hall. She leaped into the air, her black hair whipping around her face. An arc of blue light flashed from between her hands before she let it loose.

It hit three Gek'Dragar and tossed them into the air.

The knight hit the floor, rolled, and flew into the fight.

Another Gek'Dragar appeared out of the darkness, sprinting at them like a linebacker. Kennedy lifted her blaster and fired. And kept firing.

She slowed him down, but he lifted an arm like a shield, deflecting her blaster bolts.

Kennedy gritted her teeth. *Dammit.*

Her gaze fell on the floor, on the dropped Gek'-Dragar sword. She tossed the blaster and snatched up the sword.

She needed both hands to lift the thing. Damn it was huge and heavy.

But she hoisted it, just as the attacking Gek'Dragar lunged at her.

The sword pierced a joint in his armor, impaling him.

He froze, staring at her with glowing, green eyes.

Kennedy gave a heave, and shoved the sword deeper with a grunt.

He fell like a chopped tree.

Letting go of the sword, she spun back to Ashtin.

With relief, she saw he'd pushed up into a crouch, but still didn't look steady.

She dropped to her knees in front of him. "Take it easy." She cupped his cheeks, assessing.

Blue eyes met hers. "You...protected me."

Her throat suddenly got tight. Damn, she'd only met him yesterday, and already this man was getting under her skin. "Yes. I couldn't just let them kill you, Galahad."

"That is not my name."

"It's the name of a do-gooder knight in stories from Earth."

Suddenly, the hall lights came on.

Kennedy blinked and helped Ashtin to his feet.

The Grand Hall was a mess. Terrified and injured guests were crawling out of their hiding places.

"Oh, God, Douglas and Claudine." Kennedy scanned around, then spotted them. The ambassador had his arm around his wife. They were disheveled, but unharmed.

The windows were broken, the floor smashed, tables overturned.

The Gek'Dragar were either dead or gone.

Ashtin stiffened.

"Ashtin?" Kennedy said.

"Where is Knightqueen Carys?"

Gasping, Kennedy turned, taking in every inch of the room.

There was no sign of the queen.

"Maybe her knightguards got her away to safety?" Kennedy said.

"She wouldn't have left," Ashtin said. "She would have fought."

"The queen's been taken," someone yelled.

Ashtin made a choked sound.

Kennedy's stomach clenched. *Oh, fuck.*

CHAPTER SIX

Fighting off the lingering aftereffects of the Gek'Dragar weapon, Ashtin limped across the hall.

Kennedy kept pace beside him.

She was unhurt.

She'd protected him.

He'd been afraid she'd be injured, facing down the Gek'Dragar. But she hadn't faltered.

He'd gotten to see up close how brave these Terrans could be.

"Slow down or you'll fall down," she said.

"I'm fine." But he slowed his pace and glanced at her. There was blood on her skin at the top of her arm. He sucked in a breath. "You're hurt." He could see it was from a Gek'Dragar horn or claw. He touched her shoulder and saw a part of her dress was shredded... The gaping fabric revealed the slope of one of her breasts.

He mentally cursed. Now was not the time to get aroused.

"It's just a scratch." She touched his wrist. "We need to find the knightqueen."

He gave a short nod.

He saw Davion and Gayel, and Knightmaster Nea.

The female knight was a friend, and a skilled fighter. She'd been off-planet for several weeks, patrolling the borders. Searching for Gek'Dragar.

"Ashtin," Nea said.

"Nea." They clasped hands.

The female knight's aquamarine gaze moved to Kennedy. The women eyed each other.

"This is Sub-Captain Kennedy Black of Earth," he said. "Kennedy, Knightmaster Nea Laurier."

"Hi," Kennedy said.

Nea inclined her head, her expression one of urgency. "Ashtin, the Gek'Dragar took the knightqueen."

He froze, ice coating him. He cursed. "This entire attack was so they could abduct her."

"I think so."

"How did they breach Oron?" he demanded. "Let alone Aravena and the castle." He knew for a fact that the castle was heavily guarded.

"They had help," Nea said darkly.

He watched Kennedy frown.

"Ashtin, are you all right?" King Gayel's voice echoed across the Hall.

Gayel, Alea, Eve, and Davion strode toward them. All four were still clad in their Eon armor.

"Kennedy." Eve moved to Kennedy and hugged her.

"The Gek'Dragar have taken Knightqueen Carys," Ashtin said.

Both Eon warriors' faces darkened.

"By Ston's sword, how did they get in here?" Gayel asked. "And what was the weapon they used on the knights?"

"I don't know," Ashtin said. But those were both questions he wanted answered.

"They had a device that let out a blast of green light," Kennedy said. "When it hit, all the knights collapsed."

Nea scowled. "I heard a rumor. I didn't want to believe it was real." She blew out a breath. "They've found a way to affect our *oralite* implants."

Kennedy frowned. "*Oralite* implants?"

Gut churning, Ashtin met Nea's gaze. Every knight had an *oralite* implanted in them. It powered all their combat implants, and gave them enhanced abilities.

If the Gek'Dragar had found a way to short-circuit that...

By the coward's bones.

"Where's Sten?" Ashtin said. "And the other knightguards?"

Several knightguards hurried over. They were battered and splattered with blood.

"Knightmaster." The most senior guard bowed his head. "There is no sign of Knightguard Sten."

"He's gone?" There was no way Sten would abandon the queen. Hope surged. "Maybe he got Carys to safety?"

Another knightguard stepped forward. His young face was covered in sweat and blood. "I saw Sten attack several Gek'Dragar. He was protecting the knightqueen."

Frustrated murmurs moved through the knights and guards.

"And?" Ashtin prompted.

"Sten tied himself to the Queen with a dura-binding"

Gasps echoed around the hall.

"What's a dura-binding?" Kennedy asked.

"It's an unbreakable tether," Ashtin told her. "It can't be cut off without killing the two people tied to it."

Kennedy's eyes widened.

"Gek'Dragar took the queen and Sten." The young knightguard bowed his head. "I tried to reach them, but I was knocked back."

The Gek'Dragar had Carys.

"I want all available knights and guards scouring the castle and city," Ashtin ordered. "Find them."

"Knightmasters?" Someone yelled from across the room. "This Gek'Dragar is still alive."

Ashtin strode over. He spotted the alien slumped against the wall, badly hurt and bleeding. Its breaths were coming in pained rasps.

"Secure him." Anger burned in Ashtin. These aliens had taken his queen, attacked the heart of Oron.

After centuries of peace, they'd shattered it.

He crouched. "Why did you come here?"

The Gek'Dragar lifted his head. The ridges on his face looked stark, but his green eyes glowed brightly. "We will take all your planets. They are rightfully ours. You killed us in the wars. Now, we are mighty and the Oronis are weak. You won't withstand the might of the Gek'Dragar."

Ashtin's hand flexed.

"We will take your resources, your mines, your treasures." His forked tongue flicked out. "We'll take it all. Starting with your queen."

Anger flashed and Ashtin wanted to kill the interloper.

Then he felt a hand on his shoulder.

"We need to question him," Kennedy said in a steady tone.

Her voice calmed him, helped him rustle up some control. He rose. "Knightguards, take him to the cells. He's to be interrogated. I want to know *how* they infiltrated Aravena, and their plans for the knightqueen."

The Gek'Dragar laughed, a phlegmy sound. "I can tell you that already. The knightqueen is already off your planet and far from your reach. By taking her, we break your will, your spirit. We break your very backbone. As for infiltrating your precious planet and castle." He pulled out a comp device. It was slim and flat, but nothing like the ones on Oron. It was filled with schematics and information.

He saw the map of the castle and his jaw tightened.

Then Ashtin heard Kennedy suck in a sharp breath. He looked at her and frowned.

"The Terrans helped us." The Gek'Dragar smiled at Kennedy.

She shook her head. "No. That's not true!"

Ashtin felt as though the ground shifted beneath his feet. He'd started to trust Earth. Trust *her*.

"No one from my planet would help them." She lifted her chin. "He's lying."

"Is that an Earth device?" Ashtin asked, his voice sharp.

Kennedy met his gaze but didn't reply.

"Sub-Captain?"

Her jaw tightened. "Yes. It's from Earth."

KENNEDY PACED the large room with jerky strides.

The Gek'Dragar were setting Earth up. Making them look responsible for the attack and abduction of the knightqueen.

She reached the wall, spun, and strode back. Beep hovered behind her, following her path.

Douglas stood at the windows of the room they'd been stashed in, hands clasped behind his back. Claudine was pensive, fidgeting in a large chair. Eve and Davion were sitting on a couch, Kane asleep beside them, covered by a blanket. Apparently, the kid could sleep through anything.

Kennedy was well aware there were two knights standing guard outside the door.

"Kennedy, take a breath," Eve said.

"No." She swiveled and kept pacing. "I'm mad. I don't even know these Gek'Dragar." Except for the fact that a few of them had tried to kill her. "And they're framing Earth to take the fall for this. Ruining our alliance before it's even had a chance to start."

After the Kantos aliens had tried to invade and annihilate Earth, they'd learned that they were small and not as technologically advanced as many other species. They needed alliances with stronger friends.

"I know that Space Corps is not involved in this,"

Davion said. "But what are the chances someone unscrupulous on your planet is involved?"

Kennedy stopped, frowning at the floor. God, the way Ashtin had looked at her.

She'd seen betrayal in his eyes.

Her stomach pinched into knotted points. "I can't rule that out completely," she said unhappily. Beep nudged against her cheek, like he was offering comfort.

"But it is unlikely," Davion said. "Space Corps controls and regulates your space travel. Private companies aren't leaving Earth's solar system, or dealing with other species."

"Yes, but I can't prove that." Kennedy waved a hand. "Especially not to a bunch of pissed-off knights whose queen is missing."

"What a damn mess." Douglas shook his head. "I hope Knightqueen Carys is all right."

The door slammed open. Ashtin strode in, his face looking as though it was carved from a block of ice. There was no sign of the man who'd danced with her. Kissed her.

This was the knightmaster.

A knight on a mission.

The dark-haired female knight, Nea, was with him. Kennedy felt a stab of something unpleasant, slicing up to her diaphragm. The woman was striking, with high cheekbones and aqua-blue eyes. The pair looked good together. It was clear they knew each other well.

Were they a couple?

None of your business, Kennedy. Plus, he's a knight

with a creed of honor. I'm pretty sure he doesn't kiss other women if he's taken.

Oh, and he thinks you're a traitor, so he's not interested in you, anyway.

She pressed her lips together.

"The knightqueen?" Davion asked.

Ashtin's jaw tightened. "Gone. We've scoured the city, but she's not here. A ship left in the right timeframe and disappeared. We haven't been able to track it or detect it."

"Fuck," Eve muttered.

"We're *not* involved in this," Kennedy said.

Knightmaster Nea made a derisive sound.

"Look, I don't know you," Kennedy said. "So, you don't get to condemn Earth, an entire planet keen to make an alliance, because of one stupid tablet."

"Our queen is gone," Ashtin said tersely. "She is in the hands of our enemy." There was a terrible darkness in his eyes.

Kennedy swallowed. "And I'm sorry for that."

"Right now, we have no way to find her." His hand flexed.

Kennedy cleared her throat. "I fought those aliens." Now his head snapped up, his gaze electric on hers. "They are no friends of mine." She waved to her now bandaged shoulder. It was just visible under the sleeve of the shirt she'd changed into.

She saw his eyes darken with some emotion.

"It could all be a part of the setup," Nea said. "To trick us."

"Look, lady—"

"That's Knightmaster Nea to you, traitor," the other woman said.

Beep rose up and hovered in Nea's face, making a long series of beeps.

"What in the gul?" Nea snapped.

"Beep." Kennedy held up her hand and her drone plopped down on her palm. "Be nice." She lifted her head. "We are *not* involved. To prove it, let us help."

"Help?" Ashtin said.

"Yes." Kennedy straightened, slipping Beep into his holster. "We'll help get Knightqueen Carys back."

His frown deepened. "We don't have any leads—"

"I need to see the tablet," Kennedy said. "And the details of the ship that left the planet."

The two knights traded a glance.

"I assume you're questioning the Gek'Dragar?" Kennedy continued.

"Of course," Ashtin replied.

"He must know more than he's saying."

Nea was studying Kennedy carefully.

Kennedy wrinkled her nose. "We aren't as technologically advanced as you guys, but we're smart."

"And honorable and courageous," Davion added.

Kennedy smiled at the Eon warrior.

Silence fell for an agonizing moment.

"I will let you help only because of the War Commander's recommendation," Ashtin said.

Yes. Kennedy kept her face blank. She needed to do something to help. Something to prove Earth's innocence.

"Ambassador, Mrs. James," Ashtin said. "I suggest you get some rest."

"And I'd better get my little guy to a proper bed," Eve said.

Davion touched his son's head, then kissed his mate. "I'll go and check in with Gayel."

They all filed out.

Ashtin caught Kennedy's arm and dragged her closer.

"My duty is to my people, my queen."

"I know. And I want to help get her back." God, she could smell his crisp scent, with some darker undertone.

He leaned closer, and his gaze flicked to her mouth, then hardened. "If I find out you've betrayed us..."

"We haven't," she snapped. "Now, how about we get to work so we can find your queen?"

CHAPTER SEVEN

A shtin watched Kennedy study the data on the device. She was bent over the table, absorbed. She had a small furrow in her brow. Every now and then she tapped some notes onto her own tablet.

His gaze dropped, and he couldn't help but notice the way her shapely ass filled out her black pants.

Her drone rose up silently beside her, focused on him. He could swear Beep was scowling at him.

Ashtin stifled a low growl and turned away. She was a possible traitor to his people. Responsible for Knightqueen Carys being in danger.

By the coward's bones. He hoped Carys and Sten were unharmed.

Ashtin blew out a breath. The Gek'Dragar wanted Carys for a reason. At least Sten was with her. They had to hold on to hope.

Ashtin was duty-bound to find them, and take down the enemy.

His gaze was drawn back to Kennedy. She was

tapping a finger on the table, staring at the device intensely. It seemed that intensity bled over into everything she did.

He thought of the way she'd protected him, fought without hesitation against a bigger foe.

She'd taken his breath away. Was it all a ruse? A way to gain his trust?

She looked up and caught his gaze.

He cleared his throat. "Have you found anything?"

She straightened. "Are you going to believe what I tell you?"

"That depends."

She scowled. "I'm not your damn enemy, Ashtin. I want your queen back, and I want to know how an alien species that I know *nothing* about has managed to damage the reputation of my planet." She blew out a breath. "This tablet is from Earth. The star maps on here are beyond anything we have in all of Space Corps' database. You can check with Space Corps yourself. There are maps of places we don't even have the capability to travel to yet."

"Maybe that's what you traded your assistance for."

She made an angry sound. "Are you always this cold and distrusting?"

"Yes."

She rolled her eyes and looked back at the tablet. She started tapping again. Then she straightened.

He stepped closer. He smelled that sweet scent of hers again. *Honeysuckle.* "What is it?"

"Nothing. Yet. What was the ship that left the planet?"

"It was a Rimean freighter." He gritted his teeth. "It disappeared once it left Oron."

"Can I see the data you have on it?"

He nodded. He'd needed to keep an eye on her and make sure she didn't step out of line.

A part of him had no problem spending time with her. He mentally cursed himself. He needed to remember his duty.

"Ashtin," a deep voice said from behind him.

He barely controlled his jolt. He was used to Kaden sneaking up on him.

Kennedy gasped, her head whipping up.

The knighthunter emerged from the shadows at the edge of the room.

Kennedy just stared and Ashtin fought back a scowl.

Kaden was his best friend, and Ashtin was well aware that women were drawn to the knighthunter when he deigned to step into the light. It wasn't often.

Kaden was about Ashtin's height, but a little broader. He kept his platinum-blond hair cut short, and his face was sharp angles and eyes of a dark green.

"Kaden. Thanks for coming."

"Our queen is missing, and you asked. You know I'll always come."

Ashtin held an open palm to his forehead.

Kaden copied the move, then they hugged, slapping each other's backs.

"Who's this?" Kaden asked, studying Kennedy.

Unconsciously, Ashtin took a step closer to her. "Sub-Captain Kennedy Black of Earth, this is Knighthunter Kaden Galath."

"Knighthunter?" She looked Kaden up and down. "Spy." She cocked her head. "Assassin."

Kaden's lips quirked. "Take your pick." He paused. "So, you worked with the Gek'Dragar to abduct our Knightqueen."

"*No*. My planet is being framed by your enemies, to stop our alliance. Stop us working together." Her gaze narrowed. "Why would they do that? Maybe because we could help you."

Kaden nodded his head. "I agree."

Kennedy made a surprised sound. "Funny. You're more trusting than our rigid knightmaster, here."

Ashtin stiffened, but Kaden smiled. "Oh, he was born rigid."

And he'd been honed by his childhood. Both he and Kaden had been abandoned children, raised together in a home. They'd had no family name, no role models to learn from, no loving relatives to nurture them.

They'd looked up to the knights they'd see patrolling the streets.

The strong, courageous knights whose names were sung about in the songs.

A young Ashtin, who'd been nobody, had dreamed that his name would be sung about. That one day, he'd be a knight, be *somebody*.

Like Kaden, he lived for the knight's creed. To protect the knightqueen and the Oronis.

They both knew they were weapons.

Beep appeared, flying closer to Kaden.

"And who are you?" Kaden asked with a faint smile.

"Beep," Kennedy said. "My drone."

The knighthunter held up a finger. Beep hovered, then bumped against him. Ashtin frowned. The *gul-vexed* drone seemed to like Kaden.

"So, Terran," Kaden said. "Why did the Gek'Dragar want to drive a wedge between us?"

"It's a good question." Kennedy looked down at the tablet.

Ashtin didn't like Kaden watching her so intently. He moved closer behind her and shot his friend a look.

Kaden raised a brow and looked amused.

His friend activated his comms implant and spoke directly to Ashtin's implant, so that Kennedy couldn't hear.

A little territorial over the attractive sub-captain from Earth, my friend? That's not like you.

She's my responsibility. And she's a traitor.

You don't really believe that, or rather, you don't want to.

I'll do my duty.

I never doubted that, Ashtin.

We have to find Carys. The longer she's missing...

Any amusement drained out of Kaden's hawkish face, leaving behind a dark, deadly glint to his eyes.

Neither of them needed to finish that thought.

"I've got something!" Kennedy cried.

Ashtin leaned over her shoulder. "What?"

"The ship that left Oron. The reason you lost the trail is because it has a stealth camouflage generator."

Ashtin shook his head. "No. We didn't detect a stealth field. Our ships have highly advanced stealth modes. We know what to look for."

"You didn't detect anything because your stealth systems are *too* fancy." She poked him in the chest. "It looks like this one is more similar to the experimental one on our ship. It's new, and we're still testing it, but I spent most of the trip here learning how it works." She paused. "I'm pretty sure the *Helios'* chief engineer was ready to throw me out an airlock because I asked her so many questions. It's more rudimentary than yours, and the Gek'Dragar look to be using something similar."

Kaden crossed his arms.

Ashtin pressed a palm to the table and his arm brushed hers. He saw her stiffen. He still felt the spot where she'd poked him.

"Do you think your ship can track the Rimean freighter?" he asked.

Her gray gaze narrowed. "I don't know yet, but I'm sure as hell going to try."

KENNEDY'S EYES WERE BLEARY. She was on the *Helios*, working with Captain Attaway's crew. The navigation officer and chief engineer looked just as tired as she felt.

They'd worked for hours trying to find a way to

detect the ion trail left by the stealth generator on the Rimean freighter.

So far, they didn't have anything workable.

The sun was rising on Oron. Even Beep had abandoned her a few hours ago in order to recharge in their cabin. She rubbed her eyes, then snatched up her mug of coffee and sipped. She winced. It was stone cold.

"Progress?"

Ashtin's voice made her jerk and spill coffee on her wrist. "Would you knights make some noise when you move, please?"

He was dressed all in black again. It suited him. He looked hot and that annoyed her.

"I'm trained not to," he said dryly. "Have you found a way to track the ship?"

"Not exactly," Kennedy said. "We can detect the trail, but not for very far. It's a little different to the stealth mode on the *Helios*."

"But with some time and testing, we can rig up something," Chief Engineer Watson said. The older woman was one of the best engineers in Space Corps.

"Time is the one thing we don't have," Ashtin said. "Do you have any idea where the ship was headed?"

Kennedy knew how desperate he was for any lead to follow to find his queen.

"All we can say for sure is that this was its initial path." She touched the console.

A map image appeared on screen, showing the path the ship had taken off the planet.

Ashtin scowled. "It headed past the Kreora moon."

The trail petered out to nothing. They just didn't

have a way to stabilize the tracking field yet. "Then they moved out of range, and we don't have the capability to track them. *Yet.* I have every belief Chief Engineer Watson here will get our equipment tracking it."

Watson sniffed and nodded.

Knighthunter Kaden appeared like he'd popped out of nowhere.

"Jeez." The female navigation officer beside Kennedy jerked, staring at the man.

Yes, the knighthunter was an interesting man. The silver-blond hair, the sharp cheekbones, and luscious mouth all invited a woman to stare. And fantasize.

Still, it seemed she preferred darker looks and piercing blue eyes. She made herself *not* look at Ashtin.

Besides, every instinct Kennedy had told her Knighthunter Kaden was dangerous.

"Sub-Captain," Kaden drawled.

The man made her feel like a mouse being toyed with by a smug cat. Not because he was hungry, but because he could. "Knighthunter Kaden."

She saw Ashtin's scowl deepen. God, did the man know how to smile? What was he like when he wasn't wearing his armor?

The image of him naked popped into her brain.

No, you're not thinking of the knightmaster naked. God, she was tired. She rubbed her face. "We'll keep working on the—"

Footsteps. Knightmaster Nea hurried onto the bridge of the *Helios.*

"And now we're having a party," Kennedy muttered.

Nea spotted Kaden and jerked to a halt. "When did you arrive?" Her tone wasn't friendly.

Kennedy hid a smile. It was nice not to be the only hated person in the room.

"A few hours ago." A slow smile crossed Kaden's face. "As always, it's a pleasure to see your beautiful face, Nea."

The female knight sniffed and turned away, but Kennedy noted that she didn't entirely turn her back to the knighthunter. She was keeping him in her peripheral vision.

"Kennedy believes that with time and some work, this Terran ship can track the stealth field of the Rimean freighter," Ashtin said.

Nea's eyebrows rose. "Really? That's convenient."

Kennedy rolled her eyes. "Do you want our help or not?"

"Perhaps we won't need it," Nea said, a smile blooming. "I interrogated the Gek'Dragar prisoner. He gave me the name of the planet where the ship carrying the knightqueen was headed."

"Where?" Ashtin demanded.

"Cinoth."

Ashtin's lips flattened.

"Where is Cinoth?" Kennedy asked.

"At the edge of Oronis space." He clasped his hands behind his back. "It's a wild jungle planet. Overgrown and dangerous. It has some old Oronis ruins from our earliest ancestors."

"It's in the opposite direction to this trail." Nea waved at the screen. "So either you're lying or—"

Kennedy huffed out a breath. "I'm *trying* to help. But if you think it's a ruse, feel free to ignore it and perhaps risk your knightqueen."

"It's a common Gek'Dragar tactic," Kaden said. "They always start heading in the wrong direction, before they shift to their actual course."

"We have no solid proof that Carys and Sten were on the ship," Ashtin said. "Cameras at the spaceport were tampered with."

"We can't risk our queen's life," Nea said.

"We need to do both," Kaden said. "Follow the trail *and* check out Cinoth."

"I can take the *Helios* and follow the trail," Kennedy said.

"No," Ashtin snapped.

She crossed her arms. "You have to start trusting me eventually, Ashtin."

"There will be Oronis knights aboard the *Helios*." Ashtin paused. "I will go to Cinoth."

"Cinoth is dangerous," Kaden said. "If a large team lands on the planet, it'll alert the queen's abductors, not to mention the local wildlife. Even the plants are aggressive. Better to have a small team sneak onto the planet. Two people at most."

"I'm aware, Kaden," Ashtin said. "I did my trials on Cinoth."

Kennedy was really sick of not knowing what they were talking about. "Trials? Explain."

"The Knight trials. It is a quest a knight must complete to test their skills. That's how you become a knightmaster." Ashtin looked at the screen. "We all pick a dangerous planet to test us. I know Cinoth well."

"And what if there's more manufactured evidence that Earth is involved?" Kennedy said. "I don't trust the Gek'Dragar not to do more to frame us. I'm going with you to Cinoth."

"No." Ashtin straightened.

"Yes. Plus, if the Gek'Dragar deploy that weapon again, you need someone who is not Oronis to watch your back."

She could practically see Ashtin's brain ticking over. Trying to find a reason to exclude her.

"She makes some good points," Kaden murmured.

Ashtin shot his friend a look sharp enough to cut. But then he reluctantly nodded.

Kennedy hid her smile, but it was tough. She'd gotten him to agree. And now she'd get to visit a new planet no Terran had ever stepped foot on.

God, she hoped to hell they found Knightqueen Carys there and cleared Earth's name.

"So, we have two teams," Ashtin said. "Kaden and Nea will come aboard the *Helios* and follow the stealth ion trail."

The female knight stiffened. "I can work with the Terran crew alone. I don't need Knighthunter Kaden. I'm sure he has other places to be."

"We need our best working together on this." He shot Nea a look until the female knight nodded. Then he turned to Kennedy. "Kennedy and I will go to Cinoth. We'll take a small shuttle."

She pulled in a breath. "Let's go then."

"The planet is deadly. You'd better be prepared, Sub-Captain."

"I can keep up, Knightmaster. I've already saved your life once."

Kaden snickered.

"Prepare. We'll leave in an hour. I'll meet you at my ship." Ashtin turned and stalked off the bridge.

Kennedy's heart rate spiked. The upside was that she'd get to see a new planet.

The downside was being with a knight who got under her skin and believed she was a traitor. She felt a small sting under her heart.

Hopefully she could salvage the alliance with the Oronis, and bring Knightqueen Carys home safely.

And not punch a stubborn, rigid knightmaster in the face while she was at it.

CHAPTER EIGHT

Ashtin touched the controls of his ship. It wasn't the same as his large combat cruiser, the *BlackBlade*. No, it was a smaller, sleeker spacecraft, perfect for a quick and quiet infiltration. It was only himself and Kennedy aboard.

He glanced sideways. She'd napped for a few hours, and now sat in the molded, black seat beside him in a black-and-white spacesuit that fit her small, curvy body well. Her brown hair was pulled back in a tight tail. She was busy studying data on a tablet, and making her own notes. It appeared the woman lived to record everything she observed.

Beep hovered silently in the air nearby. The small drone seemed to be in standby mode. It hadn't moved or made a noise for a long time.

Kennedy shifted in her seat, tapping at her tablet.

Was she a traitor?

His gut went rock hard. He didn't want to believe it. By the coward's bones, he didn't believe it.

But he didn't have the luxury of just trusting his gut instinct. He was an Oronis knight. Duty and honor were the core of who he was. He couldn't risk them for attraction or desire.

Laughter came from the tablet.

"Sorry." She swiped the screen.

"What is that?"

She touched her hair. "A message from home."

"Your parents?" He was curious to know more about her.

"No, my parents are dead." Her voice was laden with emotion.

He didn't have parents, so he didn't have any first-hand knowledge of what losing them might feel like. "I'm sorry."

"It was a long time ago. I was twelve. They were archeologists, explorers. They died on an expedition."

Ashtin frowned. "They left their child to go on expeditions?"

"All the time." She cleared her throat. "I lived with my aunt after they died. She'd just gotten married. I was grateful they took me in. This was a message from my younger cousins." She smiled, then turned to him. "Do you have family? Siblings?"

"No."

A beat of silence.

"Ashtin, this is a chance to act a little like a normal person, less cool knight. Share a little."

"I have no parents. I was found abandoned as an infant."

"Oh, God." She looked stricken.

He shrugged. "It's just a fact. I found a family with the knights. I found duty and honor." He felt her watching him.

"What do you do for yourself?"

"I work. For Oronis and my queen."

Now Kennedy stared at him. "I mean what do you do for you. For fun and relaxation."

He met her gaze. "Serving my queen and doing my duty is for me, Kennedy. It fulfils something inside me."

"I get that. I get a lot of satisfaction from my work, and knowing it helps my planet. But there are things I do just for me."

"Like what?"

"I take photos and notes. I attend courses. I learn new things. I have some of my parents' sense of adventure running in my veins. I love seeing new places and cultures. I love finding the perfect shot that represents that. To capture a moment in time. A memory."

This woman couldn't be a traitor. His hands tightened.

Work. Focus on your mission.

Your knightqueen needs you.

"I'll send data on the planet Cinoth to your console," he told her.

She touched the console in front of her. Data projected up in a curve around her. She gasped. There were images of the jungle planet, and its flora and fauna.

"God. Some of these animals... You said it was dangerous."

"And I meant it. We can at least breathe there, the atmosphere is fine."

"You spent time there, so it makes sense I follow your lead."

He shot her a glance.

"I'm not stupid," she said.

He was very aware of that. "We'll scan the planet for activity. Find where the ship landed, and go in. If we're lucky, we'll find the knightqueen."

"I hope so." Kennedy swiped through the data. "And these ruins on the planet are Oronis?"

Her image showed the crumbled ruins of an old temple.

"Yes, but they are very old. From a time with few records. We'd like to study them more, but the planet is too dangerous to stay for very long. Once anything attacks us, it's like all the plants and animals on the planet communicate. They'll all come at us."

"Lucky us."

"When I did my trial, I had to be as stealthy as possible. But then I accidentally stepped in the nest of a small feline creature called a *truma*. It attacked, and I fought it off." And had been covered in scratches. "Then I was bombarded by attacks by other animals."

"How did you survive?"

"I ended up hiding in the half-buried roots of a tree, covered in mud to hide my scent and heat, until they gave up looking. I couldn't move at all, or I'd risk attracting them."

She leaned closer. "How long?"

"Two days."

Her nose wrinkled. "I couldn't stay still that long."

"Patience is a vital skill for a knight."

"Yes, for a Space Corps officer as well." She smiled. "But I haven't quite mastered it." She eyed him. "And what do I need to know about the Gek'Dragar."

"You mean what you don't already know about them?"

He saw her face close down and he was almost sorry for his words.

"I barely know anything about them," she said. "Whether you believe that or not."

Ashtin touched the console and adjusted their course.

"God, you are so rigid," she said. "You can't assess the facts and decide for—"

He whirled toward her. "The fact is an Earth device with Aravena schematics helped the Gek'Dragar to kidnap Knightqueen Carys."

"I fought *beside* you. I saved your life." There was heat in Kennedy's eyes.

"That could've just been to gain my trust."

"Damn you, Ashtin." She leaped out of her seat and leaned over him. "I'm *not* working with the Gek'Dragar."

"Your word isn't enough, Kennedy. Not when so much is at stake."

Beep flared to life, whirling closer and letting out a shrill beep.

"Stay out of this, Beep." She glared at Ashtin. "Dammit. You are so distrusting."

He rose, his chest pressed to hers. "I'm cautious."

"You make me so angry. Do I need to bleed for you, die for you, for you to believe—?"

The thought of this woman bleeding or dead made his body lock. He gripped her biceps.

"There will be *no* dying."

Beep butted against the side of his head.

"Beep, back," Kennedy said.

Ashtin ignored the drone, his entire focus on her. He couldn't stop himself. He leaned down and kissed her.

Her body jolted, then she was kissing him back. Ashtin groaned. The taste of her hit his tongue, the connection between them blazed like a solar flare. He felt like he'd been waiting for this, for her, and had never known it.

She threw her arms around his neck, biting his bottom lip. "We shouldn't be doing this."

"I know." He nibbled her jaw, her neck.

She moaned.

He took her mouth again. He'd never been led astray by his desire for a woman before. Never wanted one like this.

She tugged him closer and he dragged her up, off her feet. She curled one leg around his hip, and he palmed her toned ass. She rubbed against his hardening cock.

He muttered a curse. "Kennedy—"

The console chimed. It chimed again. He pressed his forehead against hers, fighting for control. They were both breathing heavily.

Reluctantly, he set her down. "I need to check that."

Beep floated nearby, swiveling between them both, like he was confused.

"Ashtin, I'm not working with the Gek'Dragar."

"I know," he said quietly.

Her brow creased. "What?"

"I know, but I need proof. My duty and honor demand it. And if I'm wrong—" he threw out a hand. "Then I'm nothing. I'd be dishonored, and I would have failed my knightqueen and my people. I'd be nothing."

Kennedy blew out a breath. "Then let's get to Cinoth and find Knightqueen Carys. I'll prove to you that Earth is not your enemy."

KENNEDY STARED AT THE PLANET. The surface was an almost-uniform, dense, dark green.

Even from a distance it looked ominous.

Ashtin's gloved hand was pressed to the controls, and she knew he was linked in, somehow. Data flowed through the projection in front of them.

"Running scans now," he said.

His deep, cool voice shivered through her. She licked her lips. She could still taste him, feel his firm lips on hers.

The man could kiss.

Focus, Kennedy. There's a killer planet right there, and you need to set foot on it.

Ashtin believed she wasn't a traitor. Or at least a part of him did. His training couldn't let him just trust his intuition. She understood that.

She rubbed her fingers on the armrest. The way he'd talked told her that he lived for being a knight. It defined him.

Did he ever let the man under the armor free?

A chime sounded. She saw him straighten.

"I found something." His gloved hand swiped through the projection. "Signs of activity in the northern hemisphere. A ship landed or took off recently."

The image of the planet zoomed in. All Kennedy could see was dense jungle, mountains, and a few pops of red. She saw that they were flowers. Giant flowers.

Beep let out a chirp from her left shoulder. "Yes, it's very wild." She looked at Ashtin. "Where the hell would a ship land?"

"I'm not sure, but it was in this area somewhere." The screen resized to show an area to the north. "Once we're on the ground, I'll take a handheld scanner." He turned to her. "On the planet, be sure to stay behind me."

Kennedy snorted.

He shot her a sharp look.

"I'll follow your lead, Knightmaster, but I won't cower behind you like a frightened little child. I'm here to help."

She saw a muscle tick in his jaw, then he turned to the console and flew them into the atmosphere.

Soon, they were flying over the canopy of giant trees. Her breath caught. The view was incredible. Through a tiny gap in the trees, and she saw a river winding like a silver snake, before it tipped over some cliffs.

"The scanner readings are being distorted by pollen in the air," he said. "Hopefully we'll be able to detect the ship on the ground."

The trees and foliage were so dense, and there was nowhere to land the ship. She studied some of the pointed mountains in the distance. Only the tops of them poked through the canopy.

Then their ship moved into a hover over the smallest clearing she'd ever seen.

Ashtin rose, his black armor sliding into place. She watched the bands of black wrap around him from behind.

She really, really wanted to take a picture of him. The knight before the mission.

"I really want to know how your armor works," she said.

He looked at her, helmet in place but visor open. "We don't share that information. All I can tell you is that we have combat implants."

"Powered by *oralite*. That the Gek'Dragar can affect with their new weapon."

"Yes."

Curiosity itched at her. "And what is *oralite*, exactly?"

"It's a nano-implant. That's all I'm saying, or I know the information will end up on your tablet."

She grinned. "I'm a xenoanthropologist. It's my job to learn and record."

He sighed. "The *oralite* grows into a knight's brainstem."

Her eyes widened. "Really?"

"And our armor has receptors built into it." He lifted his arm and tilted it. "Especially in our forearms and gloves. They help us channel energy and create what we need. A blade, a sword, balls of energy."

A million questions burst to life in her head. "And what about—?"

"No more," he said. "That's all you're getting." He headed out of the cockpit.

She'd get more answers out of him. Eventually. She rose and followed him. "So, you can land the ship in that minuscule clearing we're hovering over?"

"No. Have you got everything you need?"

She automatically checked her blaster at her hip, and the gear on her belt. "Beep, you stay aboard the ship."

The drone vibrated and let loose with a string of beeps.

"No, it's too dangerous." She stroked the side of Beep's round shell. "Stay here. Please?"

One sad beep.

"Good. I'll contact you if I need you." She looked at Ashtin. "So how are we getting down there?"

He slipped a scanner with a flat screen onto his belt, then touched a control panel set into the side of the ship. The side door slid open, and the smell of vegetation hit her.

He held out an arm. "We're jumping."

Kennedy's eyes went wide. "What?"

"Don't worry, I won't let you get hurt."

Oh. *Hell*. It was her one little weakness. She didn't like heights.

"Kennedy?" He was watching her carefully.

She steeled herself and stepped forward. *Don't look down. Don't look down.*

Ashtin curled one strong arm around her and

instantly her thoughts scattered. All she felt was his hard body, the strength of him.

"Ready?" he asked.

She swallowed. "No, but let's do it."

Before she could catch her breath, he jumped out of the ship.

Oh, freaking God. She clung to him, and buried her face in his neck.

They plummeted, and her stomach lodged somewhere in her throat.

She felt a prickle of energy, and they slowed a little. But the wind still whipped her hair around and they were falling. A long way. To the hard ground. Without a parachute.

"I won't let you get injured, Kennedy."

She opened her eyes and stared into his blue ones.

"My suit can control our fall."

"Are you sure?" she squeaked.

The faintest smile. "Yes."

"Okay." She made herself keep her eyes open. She turned her attention to the branches around them. The foliage was deep green, with the hue broken by the flash of birds taking off in flight. The trunks of the trees were immense. Thicker than buildings back home on Earth.

They slowed some more, then landed. Ashtin bent his knees, and her boots touched the dirt.

For a second, his arm tightened on her, keeping her close. Her pulse jumped. Then he released her.

She dragged in a breath and looked around. The trees soared high overhead. The undulating call of some creature echoed through the forest.

Ashtin pulled the scanner off his belt and held the device up. Lights on it blinked.

"I'm picking up some energy disturbance," he said.

She nodded. "Let's find these assholes."

They set off through the trees. She saw the cautious way he scanned the surroundings. She wasn't foolish enough to think this was just another pretty planet. She knew there were dangers lurking.

"Do we need to be silent?" she murmured.

"No. But if we attack something, then we'll trigger an aggressive response. Step lightly and keep your eyes open."

They trekked on, closer to the mountains. The vegetation grew denser, blocking out the light. There were more shadows beneath the trees. On some of the trunks, she saw neon-green sap dripping down.

"The sap is highly toxic," Ashtin warned her. "And don't eat or drink anything. Most of the water here has toxic algae in it."

"There goes my plan for a feast."

A rustle sounded, and she glanced sideways. Deep in the darkness under the shrubbery, a pair of red eyes blinked, watching them. Her hand rested on her blaster.

But the creature didn't attack. Kennedy let out a long breath.

They moved on, and suddenly, a large stone appeared. She gasped. It was pointed at the top, like an arrowhead. As they got closer, she could see engravings on the rock. They looked almost like hieroglyphs, or runes.

Ashtin stepped closer, and bowed his head. "These

are ancient Oronis stones."

"We have similar standing stones on Earth."

"These are very old. Very early Oronis. Before we became a cohesive species and solidified our beliefs and culture." He reached out and touched the stone. "But honor was still important. This symbol here is the word for honor." As he touched one of the engraved runes, light pulsed through the engravings, the same shade of blue as the energy he used in a fight.

"Wow," she breathed.

"Let's keep moving."

They moved through a stand of small trees, and not long beyond that, she noticed webs covering everything. They stretched across some of the pathways.

Very large webs.

"Try not to disturb the webs." He ducked under one.

"Should I ask what makes them?"

He gave her a faint smile. "A creature called the *ikadus*. They have four legs, no eyes, and sharp fangs. Their bodies are covered in tiny hair-like filaments that can detect movement and vibration. They're only dangerous if they perceive you as a threat."

"Roger that."

"They trap their prey in their webs, and keep them there for days, tearing strips of flesh off their bodies."

Kennedy winced.

Soon, the ground turned rockier. Thorny bushes grew at the base of the trees and she smelled rotting leaves and fragrant flowers. Looking up, she saw vines twisting around the trunks, laden with wide-petaled white blooms.

On the ground, long, tubular plants grew in vibrant colors. Her lips parted. They were so beautiful. Each tube was the size of her arm, with a flower on top. They were a gorgeous array of green, pink, white, blue, and yellow.

She leaned over one and breathed deeply. God, that lush scent was amazing. She breathed again, smiling. It smelled good, looked beautiful. She reached out and stroked the soft, velvety flower petals.

Suddenly, the tube moved. It opened and clamped onto her arm. She was yanked down, the planet swallowing her entire arm. The flower on top closed up.

"Shit!" she cried.

Ashtin whirled and cursed.

Kennedy tugged, but the plant wasn't letting go. She fumbled for the knife on her belt.

"No!" He reached her, hand pressed to her back. "Don't kill it. If you do, it might trigger the attack response from the other flora and fauna."

"It's trying to eat my arm, Ashtin!"

"It lured you in with it's scent." He felt around the plant. "We just need to get it to release you without killing it."

"Am I in danger?"

"This species contains a chemical that will slowly digest your arm. You're safe for now."

"Great," she mumbled. "I can't believe I touched it."

"That's what it's scent is designed to do." He gripped the base of the plant and squeezed.

It wriggled, clearly unhappy.

"Get ready," he warned.

Kennedy breathed through her mouth, trying to avoid any more of the plant's intoxicating scent.

He jabbed at the plant's roots. It opened up and Kennedy wrenched her arm free. She stumbled back and Ashtin caught her.

He pulled her to his chest, a hand in her hair. They watched the plant, waiting to see what it would do.

It undulated, then went still. The flower on top reopened.

"Okay?" He looked down at her.

"Yeah. Thanks, Galahad."

He tugged on her hair, then let her go.

As they continued on, Kennedy's pulse settled. She was much warier as they trekked through the vegetation.

They passed an entire group of standing stones, some of them taller than her, and all of them carved with ancient Oronis engravings.

Ashtin slowed, frowning at the runes.

"Ashtin?"

"I can't read some of these. Not all these old runes are in our database." He pressed a palm to one stone, making light ripple through the runes. "And many are too worn to make out."

She watched him carefully. Something was bothering him.

He turned to her. "They're a warning."

Chill ran down her spine. She scanned around. "A warning for what?"

He met her gaze. "I don't know."

Something told her that they really didn't want to find out.

CHAPTER NINE

The scent of rotting vegetation increased, and the sound of the birds and animals fell silent.

Ashtin heard Kennedy's quiet breathing as she followed behind him. They circled a large tree, and he stopped.

Mist swirled across the ground, and had an eerie green tinge. It curled around the tree trunks like it was alive.

Ahead was a flat patch of swampy ground. The dirt was a deep brown, and there were puddles of water here and there. A few purple flowers bloomed in it.

"No tracks through here," Kennedy murmured.

No. It seemed the jungle creatures avoided this spot.

"We could circle around," she suggested.

But the patch of swampy ground extended off on both sides, and into viciously thorned bushes. They'd lose a lot of time finding another path.

"Can you sense anything on your scanners?" she asked.

He ran a quick scan, but shook his head. "Nothing out of the ordinary." He crouched and picked up a small stick. He tossed it out onto the swamp.

Nothing happened.

"Let's move across it fast," he said, rising.

Ashtin stepped onto the soggy dirt. It was damp, but not too muddy. The mist eddied around his legs, while the dirt sucked at his boots.

As he headed across, Kennedy moved in beside him. They passed some of the purple flowers, and as he watched, they curled up and sank into the dirt.

Like they were hiding.

His jaw tightened. *Not a good sign.*

"No birds chirping," Kennedy whispered. "No animals rustling."

Then ahead, the swampy soil vibrated.

They both stopped. They were almost to the center of the swamp. Nearby, a mound formed, like something was pushing up from beneath.

"Another one to the left," she said.

Ashtin saw four separate spots bulging upward. He slid his visor into place, and he saw Kennedy pull out her blaster.

His scan couldn't penetrate the soil, whatever was under there was a mystery.

Then a scaly, bony leg shot up through one mound, tipped with a sharp claw. Another burst out of a second mound.

"Shit," Kennedy said.

"*Move.*" Ashtin ran left while Kennedy ran right.

Another leg stabbed down at him and he dodged.

Across the swamp, he saw two more long legs burst free of the dirt. Two swung toward Kennedy. She fired her blaster, laser lighting up the mist.

Gul. This *gul*-vexed creature would either kill them, or force them to kill it. Which would cause them far bigger problems.

Energy flowed from his implants, charging through his suit. His sword formed, glowing blue.

He swung at the closest leg, slicing the end of it off.

The creature below the soil let out a muffled screech, and the ground heaved.

"Go, Kennedy! Get to the other side."

She took off sprinting.

A leg swung at her, and she leaped over it.

Ashtin took off running. He jumped over a rocky patch in the middle of the swamp, his boots squelching.

Ahead, Kennedy swiveled and fired behind him. Then he saw her eyes widen.

A shadow fell over him, growing larger and larger.

He looked back. *By the coward's bones.* His chest locked.

A large monster with twelve of those long bony legs pulled itself out of the dirt. It had a bulky, bulbous body with a bony head. Its huge mouth yawned open, two sharp mandibles snapping open and closed.

He threw a ball of energy at it. When it hit the alien, the creature gave an undulating roar that echoed through the trees.

Ashtin picked up speed.

The horrid stench of rotting flesh and dead things hit

him. Then something slammed into his back. A leg had hit him. It lifted him off his feet.

He sailed through the air and hit the swampy ground, mud splattering over him.

Tentacles burst out of the soil, wrapping around him. *Gul.*

The slimy protuberances clamped on both his legs, around his middle, and one on his left arm.

He jerked and bucked, but the tentacles just tightened, half pulling him down into the swampy soil. He was stuck.

Any second, the monster would shake off its stupor and come for him.

A shot of laser hit the tentacle wrapped around his leg. It exploded, then released him, and slithered back into the dirt.

Another precision shot, and his arm was free.

A third shot and the tentacle around his middle wriggled away.

The giant swamp creature roared. It took a step and the ground rumbled.

Ashtin quickly sat up. He saw Kennedy on one knee, her blaster up and aimed.

Of course, she was a precision shot. She'd probably taken advanced training. She fired at the swamp monster while he stabbed at the final tentacle and leaped to his feet.

"Come on!" she yelled, swiveling as she kept firing at the monster.

Ashtin ran to her. Then together, they sprinted across the water-logged dirt.

"Almost there." He could see the far edge. There were giant trees ringing the swamp, some with roots exposed.

Suddenly, there was a wild screech overhead. Off to the right, the vegetation started shaking.

"Something's coming," she said.

"Don't stop."

All of a sudden, thorny vines snapped out of the ground and wrapped around Kennedy's middle.

"What the hell?" She jerked.

Ashtin formed a blue energy blade and sliced through the vine. He saw the thorns had pierced her suit in a couple places and she was bleeding.

"The planet's attack instinct had been activated," he said.

"Great. Just great."

"We need to hide." He took her hand and ran.

His gaze zeroed in on the tree roots. They'd worked for him before.

"In under those roots."

She grimaced. "Oh, no."

"Yes." He dropped to his knees and waved her in. "Get as much mud on you as you can."

Her nose wrinkled.

"You wanted to experience a new planet," he said.

"This isn't quite what I had planned in my head."

With a roar, the swamp monster headed their way. Behind it, on the other side of the swamp, Ashtin saw a pack of feline creatures with glowing gold eyes burst out of the trees. One threw its head back and howled.

The sight had Kennedy diving into the roots.

He quickly followed her.

They sank deep into the mud, and when they settled, they were pressed chest to chest against each other, half buried.

"Okay?" he asked.

"Sort of."

More animals poured into the swamp. Ashtin pulled her close and hoped they got out of this alive.

———

KENNEDY TRIED to stay still and quiet.

It wasn't easy when dangerous alien predators prowled around while you were hiding in the mud with an alien knight.

Hers and Ashtin's faces were inches apart.

"Hi," she said quietly.

"Hi."

They both whispered, not wanting to attract any attention.

"Are you hurt?" he asked.

"Just a few scratches. You?"

"I'm fine. Thanks for getting the tentacles off me."

She smiled. "Any time."

She realized they were plastered together, his arm wrapped around her hip. "Mud and killer alien animals aside, this is kind of nice," she said. "You're a pretty good hugger, Knightmaster."

It was just what she needed after the adrenaline overload of the last hour.

"I don't hug." His brow creased. "I don't think I've

ever been hugged."

Kennedy felt a pinch in her chest. "What? Never?"

"It wasn't encouraged at the home for orphans where I was raised. And once I started training to be a knight, we were too busy training."

At least she'd had caring nannies, and after she'd lost her parents, her aunt had never been stingy with hugs. Maybe there had been times when Kennedy sensed her aunt and her husband would have preferred not to start their married life with a child that wasn't theirs, but they'd still given her a home.

Ashtin hadn't had anything like that.

"You're close to Kaden."

"He grew up with me. He had no parents either." Ashtin made a small sound. "But we don't hug. We usually spar."

Men. She grinned. "Of course." But it was clear to her that the pair were almost like brothers.

She snuggled into him, ignoring the fact that they were half submerged in mud. "I'll hug you."

His hand flexed on her hip. "Kennedy—"

There was a snuffling sound and they both froze.

She saw Ashtin look past her, and slowly, she turned her head.

A stocky creature with two tusks and a wide snout was sniffing at the base of the tree where they hid. It had a gray, leathery hide. It let out several deep grunts.

Shit. Could it smell them?

"Don't move," he said near soundlessly.

Suddenly, a large, lithe feline—bigger than a lion or tiger—leaped onto the roots right by their heads. It hissed at the hog-like alien. The cat's fur was a deep black shot through with purple.

The hog grunted and charged. The feline sprang away, hissing and snarling. The animals moved off, the cat swiping at the hog.

"Can you still see the creature in the swamp?" she asked.

"It's gone now."

Thank God.

But there were still other alien animals sniffing around. She tried not to fidget.

"Stay still," he admonished.

"I'm *trying*. I warned you that I'm not good at being still." *How the hell had he stayed like this for two days?* "I've always been a fidgeter. Unless I'm reading or taking notes."

"You do that a lot."

"It started when I was young. My parents would leave on a trip, and I was always wondering when they'd get back. I needed to fill the time." She looked at his chest, all the emotions bubbling up. God, now was *not* the time.

His fingers brushed her jaw and tipped her face up.

Those fascinating blue eyes were steady on her.

"But it was more than that," he said.

She didn't like that he read her so easily. She blew out a breath. "I wanted to be with them. I thought that if I learned as much as I could, one day, they'd take me with them."

"But they didn't."

"No. And then they died. It took me a while to realize

they didn't want me with them. I would have been a nuisance and in the way of them doing what they really loved."

"Kennedy." He cupped her cheek, and felt the comforting touch of his fingers.

It seemed crazy that she could take comfort from this deadly man.

"Not loving you enough was their failing, not yours," he said.

Her heart skipped a beat.

"You are an accomplished, skilled woman. Just as you are. You don't need to be more. You're enough just as you are."

Those words burrowed deep inside. No one had ever said anything like that to her before.

Her parents had always left. Her aunt had taken her in, but she'd always felt like the outsider in her aunt's family. She'd known they were happy when she'd left to join Space Corps.

"I shouldn't be complaining," she said. "I had parents, even if they weren't always there. They loved me in their own way, as best they could. You didn't even have that."

"I survived. The Oronis care well for their abandoned and orphaned children."

That wasn't the same as having a loving family.

"Then I became a knight. I was determined to help my people, and make something of myself."

His fingers were still caressing her cheek. Suddenly, she wasn't on a dangerous jungle world, hiding in the mud.

It was just her and Ashtin.

She shifted and pressed her lips to his.

His mouth sealed over hers, his hands tightening on her. He kissed her harder, deeper, and she met every thrust of his tongue, kissing him back.

She heard a low groan escape him. She loved hearing that.

Kennedy slowed the kiss, drawing in the taste of him. He ran his tongue over her bottom lip.

Then he broke the kiss, and they stared at each other.

"Your enough too, Ashtin. You don't have to be the perfect, dedicated knight all the time." She flattened a palm over his chest, his armor slick under her skin. "You can let the man out sometimes."

He just stared at her, so much working behind his blue eyes. Then he flicked his gaze past her, and his body tensed.

"The animals are gone," he said.

That's when she realized a hush had fallen over the swamp again. Kennedy carefully turned, the mud squelching under her.

There were no deadly creatures nearby. The mist playfully danced over the swamp.

"We need to go while we can," Ashtin said. "But move slowly."

She crawled out from under the roots. Nothing moved in the bushes around them. No plants or animals attacked.

He took her hand, they moved slowly and stealthily away from the swamp.

Ashtin was alert, his body tense as he scanned the dense trees.

The mud was drying on Kennedy's space suit. She poked at the holes that the thorns had made. She'd need to repair it later. The mud was drying in her hair too. *Ick.* And it didn't smell good.

Something crashed in the vegetation behind them. Ashtin's fingers clenched on hers. A creature let out a wild, haunting howl.

"Run!" he barked.

Adrenaline spiked through her, and she took off running. They crashed through the bushes, then found a narrow path through the trees.

Ashtin sprinted ahead and she pushed to keep up with him. She heard creatures thundering through the bushes nearby.

God, she really didn't want to get eaten by some hungry Cinothian beast.

Another howl sounded behind them.

Close. Whatever it was it was close.

Kennedy's chest was burning. Suddenly, Ashtin stopped, slid an arm around her, then jumped.

They sailed up into the air, soaring toward the huge, sprawling branches of the trees. She gasped and clung to him.

Oh, God. Oh, God. Then she looked down.

Her stomach did a sickening swirl. They were high up. *Really* high up. Then her gaze snagged on several shaggy-haired creatures on the ground below. They were the size of a small transport, loping across the jungle floor on four powerful legs. They lifted their muzzles and sniffed.

Hunting them.

Ashtin pressed his boots to a tree trunk and rebounded them off it, propelling them forward. Leaves slapped at them. He kept driving through the tree canopy, bounding off trunks and branches.

She decided to keep her gaze locked on his strong jaw line and *not* think about how high up they were.

Then he landed on a thick branch and paused.

Kennedy pulled in a shuddering breath, holding onto him tightly. They both peered down. The jungle was quieter and there was no sign of the creatures.

"I think we lost them," she murmured.

"I'm not detecting any large lifeforms nearby." He leaped off and they arrowed downward.

She closed her eyes. When their boots hit the ground, she was pretty damn happy.

That's when she saw the webs.

They were all around them, strung between the trees and dangling overhead.

"Um, you're not detecting any—" what had he called them? "—*ikadus* nearby?"

"No. But they don't always show up on scans. When they're still, they shut down most of their bodily functions so their potential prey can't detect them."

Kennedy squeezed her eyes closed for a second. "After heights, I dislike spiders the most."

"They aren't really spiders. They only have four legs."

She shot him a look. "Oh, well that makes it so much better."

His lips moved into a half smile. "I'll protect you."

"Thanks, Galahad."

He touched her mud-caked hair and gave it a tug.

They set off, moving cautiously through the dense webs. Ashtin carefully cut a path through, trying not to disturb the webs too much.

Some of the sticky stuff got in her hair and she plucked it off.

Covered in mud and webs. *Nice.*

She ducked under some more webs, then heard Ashtin curse softly. She spun.

He was caught in a dense web, one of his arms out to the side and the other close to his body. He jerked to get free, the web rocking.

"Hang on." She moved to him and pushed on the web. "It's really sticky."

"That means its freshly made."

She stilled and met his gaze. "You really didn't need to mention that." She tried to pull his arm free. "God, you're really stuck."

"Cut it."

Nodding, she pulled her knife off her belt. She sliced at the web, but it was really hard to cut. She sawed the blade through it.

That's when she saw two red eyes blink on in the shadows behind Ashtin.

Her stomach plunged to her feet. "*Ashtin...*"

He tensed. "Its biosign just flared to life. Stay still. Don't move."

The *ikadus* unfurled from its hiding spot in the hollow of a tree trunk. Its four legs were long and jointed, and it had a spider-like appearance. It was a little larger than

Ashtin, no eyes on its smooth head, but several fangs protruded from its mouth. Fangs designed for ripping flesh. It moved slowly and looked like it was covered in gray fur, but she realized it was the filaments it used to sense motion.

Barely breathing, she stood still, looking back at Ashtin.

Her knight looked calm. His gaze stayed on her.

For a second, it was just the two of them...until the *ikadus* shifted closer.

Her heart thumped painfully hard in her chest. God, it was *right* there. Only a thin sheet of web separated her from the creature. She winced, trying not to look at those fangs.

It circled around them, pausing a few times.

Then it moved away. She watched it climb up the massive tree trunk and disappear.

"*God.*" She released a shaky breath.

"Cut the web, Kennedy."

"Right." She sliced him free.

He cupped her face. "Thanks. You did well."

"I was screaming on the inside."

He lowered his head and her chest hitched. He pressed the lightest kiss to her lips. "Come on, we need to find where that ship landed."

He took her hand and set off through the trees. After a few minutes, her system evened out, her racing pulse slowing. Nothing seemed to be chasing them.

The ground grew rockier and rockier.

"I think we're safe now." He paused and pulled out his handheld scanner.

"Ugh, we're a mess." She swiped at the caked mud all over her.

"I can clean you off," he said.

Her eyebrows rose. "Really?"

He nodded and stepped closer. "Hold still."

His palms cupped her shoulders. She felt a pulse of energy, the hairs on the back of her neck rising. Blue light, less intense than when he was fighting, glowed on his palms.

The energy pulsed over her, and as she watched, the mud dried and flaked off.

"Oh," she murmured.

The blue energy ran over him, leaving his armor clean.

She reached up and touched her hair. It was silky and clean. "Neat trick."

"Come on. The trail leads this way." He motioned with the scanner.

They needed to find the knightqueen. And avoid getting eaten by any wildlife.

Soon, Ashtin stopped at a smooth cliff face that rose high above them.

Kennedy arched her head back, marveling at the massive cliffs. The rocks here were a deep brown, criss-crossed by some golden veins that glinted in the light.

"Where now?" she asked.

He frowned at the scanner and studied the cliff face. "The trail ends."

She stilled. "There's nothing here."

CHAPTER TEN

His jaw tight, Ashtin studied the wall, then the scanner screen again. "I'm detecting the residual energy signature. Someone was here."

"They can't have just disappeared." Kennedy marched up to the wall, and pressed her hands to the brown stone. "I don't see a doorway."

Ashtin frowned. "They passed by here."

She arched her head, looking up. "Do you think they climbed? Or flew up? Maybe the ship is up there, somewhere?"

The cliff face was huge, and he didn't see any caves or entrances above. "I don't know."

He stepped up beside her and moved his palm across the rock.

"Wait." She paused. "There's a line here, a groove in the stone." She followed her finger along it.

"I found one, too." It was very straight, then it curved. Their fingers met. He looked at her. As their gazes meshed, he saw her pulse fluttering in the side of her neck.

His hunger for her was growing. She'd been with him every step on this planet. Had fought beside him. Saved him.

He had to stay focused on his mission.

Suddenly, he felt a pulse of energy.

"Whoa." Kennedy stumbled back in surprise, and he caught her.

Blue light lit up the grooves, running across the rock face, forming a glowing image. The carvings were intricate.

It was a whole wall of old Oronis runes.

A large one dominated the center.

"Do you know what it means?" she asked.

"Enter."

There was a rumble of sound and the rock started to move, sliding away to reveal a tall, long doorway in the cliff face.

"Holy hell," Kennedy breathed.

Ashtin summoned his energy and it crackled on his palm. He stepped inside.

Inside was a circular tunnel, with smooth sides.

Kennedy pushed up beside him. "This is *amazing*. How come your people haven't explored here?"

"Cinoth is good at hiding secrets, and as you've discovered, the planet is dangerous. And I didn't know there were ruins in the mountainside. I saw plenty dotted across the planet, mostly tumbled and weathered, when I did my trials."

The door rumbled closed behind them, leaving them

in thick, impenetrable darkness. Ashtin touched the forearm of his suit, and energy flowed through it, making the armor on his arm glow with blue light. It was enough for them to see.

They continued down the tunnel.

"Watch your step," he warned. "I've heard our historians who have studied other ancient sites say that the old Oronis were good at protecting their temples."

"So, I need to watch out for a huge, rolling boulder?"

He frowned at her. "What?"

She waved a hand. "Don't worry. It's a reference to an old Earth movie. I'll—"

With a loud rumble, the walls started shaking, and dust filtered down from the roof of the tunnel.

Suddenly, a part of the tunnel floor collapsed, falling downward.

Including the part under one of Kennedy's boots.

With a yelp, she started to fall.

Ashtin lunged forward and grabbed her hand.

She hung over the dark drop.

"Shit."

There was dense darkness below. He had no idea how deep it went, but he sensed the vastness that indicated it went a long way.

He hauled her up, pulling her close. She clung to him, and he liked it. He liked that toned, compact body fitting against his like a puzzle piece.

"Thanks." Her voice was husky.

"I told you I wouldn't let you get hurt down here, Kennedy."

"You knights would sacrifice yourself for others, right? For duty and honor."

He touched her temple and the healing scratch there. "Not for everyone."

They stared at each other for a beat. Then a low growl echoed through the tunnel.

She spun and they stared down into the hole below.

"What was that?" she murmured.

"I don't think we want to find out." Ashtin looked ahead. "We need to work out how to get across this tunnel."

"Without plunging into the deadly abyss filled with the growling thing."

He glanced at the walls, then the floor again. He could see joints between the stones. Some had fallen, others hadn't. "There must be a pattern."

Kennedy crouched, then fingered the stone. "Look. This part has two depressions." She swiped the dust off. "And there are more of those rune-like engravings."

He crouched beside her. "You're right." He traced them.

"Man, I really wish I had my tablet and could record these." She looked at him. "Can you read them?"

He activated his visor. "I'll check our databases. There's no exact match, but some are similar to Oronis runes of the Second Period. They say duty and service."

Her nose wrinkled. "Um, does that help?"

"Duty and service." He touched the two rounded depressions. Then he realized what they were for. He'd seen them in the ruins of the supplicants' temple on Nanda IV.

He shifted and placed his knees in the depressions, kneeling.

"Oh." Kennedy moved to the adjacent ones and knelt beside him.

A faint click echoed around them.

Blue light ran across the stone floor, lighting up more runes.

Kennedy's lips parted. "It's beautiful."

Ashtin rose. "It's the path we have to follow."

She nodded. "I'll go first."

He scowled. "*I'll* go first."

She smiled. "You can rescue me if I fall, Knightmaster." She stepped onto the first glowing rune.

The stone didn't fall.

As Kennedy walked slowly across, he followed close behind her.

When they safely reached the end of the tunnel, she turned and smiled at him.

Ashtin felt the violent need to kiss her. His hands flexed. No one had ever tested his control like this.

"Okay." She peered into the gloom ahead. Several tunnels split off in different directions. "Where to next?"

He lifted the scanner. "We'll—"

A loud, guttural roar echoed off the walls.

They spun, and watched as a huge, scaled creature covered in spikes pulled itself out of the abyss.

Its glowing gold eyes settled on them, then it opened its jaw full of teeth and roared.

KENNEDY STARED at the alien creature. It had brown scales, two huge horns on its head, and wicked spikes along its back. It crouched in the tunnel, drool dripping off its fangs.

Ashtin lifted a palm, and she felt energy welling around them, building up. The hairs on the back of her neck rose. The ball of energy on his palm grew.

He grabbed her arm with his other hand. "Run!" He shoved her, then threw the energy ball at the creature.

Kennedy didn't wait to see it hit. She sprinted as fast as she could. She took the middle tunnel, just as the beast roared behind her and snarled. She assumed Ashtin had hurt it.

Ashtin ran up behind her. "Left."

They swiveled and sprinted down another tunnel.

Another deafening roar reverberated along the walls, making her grit her teeth. She glanced back and saw the creature loping after them. It leaped against the wall and rebounded off it, moving fast.

Ahead, the tunnel opened into a giant, circular chamber.

There was no time to study the statues dotted around the walls. Faint light filtered down from above, casting a bluish glow across the space. In places, dark-green vines covered the walls, thick and tangled.

They spun and Kennedy yanked out her blaster. Ashtin held up his hands, and was holding a long sword that glowed with dark blue energy.

The beast slunk closer, claws scraping on the stone floor.

Shit, it was big. Its powerful body was larger than a

tiger's. It looked like a tiger and crocodile had made a baby.

A hungry, angry baby.

It leaped into the air.

Kennedy opened fire. Her blaster whined, laser lighting up the chamber.

The creature landed, shaking its head. Kennedy went down on one knee and kept firing.

Ashtin leaped into the air, his coat flaring behind him. Her heart clenched. God, he looked amazing. He lifted the sword high above his head and brought it down on the alien's back.

The beast roared. Ashtin rolled and came up on his feet.

The creature whipped around fast, and roared again. Two blue discs shot from Ashtin's hands, biting into the creature's hide.

Kennedy kept firing. Damn, its scaled hide was like armor. She wasn't doing enough damage.

The beast leaped at Ashtin.

Oh, shit. Kennedy jumped up and ran.

Ashtin spun away and shot off another blue blade.

The alien creature lunged, caught Ashtin's arm in its jaws, then tossed the knight into the air.

He sailed through the space, hit the ground and rolled. She saw him push up on his hands and knees, but he looked dazed.

The creature advanced on him.

No!

Kennedy ran and fired again. She circled around, aiming for the beast's eyes.

It threw its head back and roared.

"You don't like that, do you?" *Ashtin, get up.*

He slapped a palm to the floor and rose.

Suddenly, runes activated on the floor. Blue lines in concentric circles on the stone lit up.

He strode toward her, firing another ball of energy at the beast.

The creature dropped back, wary.

The floor shook, and Kennedy stumbled. Ashtin caught her.

Suddenly, the circular floor started to rise. The beast growled, and Kennedy fired again.

"Together," Ashtin yelled. He threw several small energy discs at the beast.

She concentrated her fire on the creature's ugly head.

It yowled, turned, then leaped off the rising platform.

"Where the hell are we going?" She looked up and could only see darkness above. Were they about to be crushed against the ceiling?

As they neared the top, the rock slid open. The platform rose into another cavern and stopped.

The blue glow of the floor stayed, running to statues at the edge of the circle. Small rings of blue fire ignited at the bases of the sculptures.

Ashtin walked to one and Kennedy gasped.

It was an Oronis knight, kneeling with his head bowed and a sword in hand. The next statue showed a tall knight, mid battle, sword raised. The next statue was a female knight standing at attention.

Then Kennedy's gaze fell on the final statue. She sucked in a breath. "It's Knightqueen Carys."

The woman looked elegant, wearing a cloak and crown, her face beautiful and haughty.

"No, this is a knightqueen of old. Carys is of the original bloodline." Ashtin strode off the platform. He pulled out his scanner. "I'm picking up recent activity. We're in the right place."

There was light in the tunnel ahead.

As her gaze followed him, it caught on drops of blood on the stone floor.

"You hurt?" She jogged over to him.

"The beast caught me." He showed her his arm, and the three nasty gashes that had cut through his armor. "It's not life-threatening."

She huffed. "What if its claws were covered in bacteria or poison? These slashes need to be cleaned."

He gave her a faint smile. "Worried about me, Sub-Captain?"

She grumbled. "Fine. Die of a weird alien infection, see if I care."

He cupped her cheek. "My combat implants will purge any infection and slow the bleeding."

"Oh. That's handy."

"You can bandage me on the ship."

"Or I can throw some bandages at your head."

His smile widened into a full-blown, gorgeous smile.

Oh. Her heart did a funny squeeze. The man was even more attractive when he smiled. She'd made this stoic, serious knight smile.

A part of her wanted to do that more often.

"Kennedy?"

She realized she was gawking at him like a love-struck teenager. "Let's keep moving."

The tunnel opened up. They were now in a huge cave cut into the side of the mountain. There was a large opening, revealing blue sky and a sea of trees below.

And, there was a small ship parked off to the side.

The Rimean freighter.

The ship that had escaped Oron.

Ashtin straightened and held his right arm out.

She watched the sword form, the blue energy moving from his palm, coalescing until the long sword rested in his hand.

It was incredible.

He looked at her. "Let's find my queen."

CHAPTER ELEVEN

Ashtin scanned the ship through his visor. It was definitely a Rimean model.

"No life signs." He'd hoped to find Carys and Sten.

Ashtin and Kennedy approached silently. She kept her blaster up and aimed.

The side ramp of the ship was open, and he walked up it. The vessel was run down, old. Its hull panels were battered and damaged. The inside wasn't much better.

He took in the curved, worn seats, missing cabinet panels, and general air of neglect. Kennedy stepped up beside him.

"Any sign the knightqueen was here?" she asked.

"Let's take a look around."

She nodded.

As she searched the passenger area, he moved to the cockpit. It was boxy and barely functional. There was no beauty in its design. It was built to lug freight.

He approached the console.

There was a whirr, and a metallic object slid out of the wall.

"Security blaster!" he yelled.

He saw Kennedy dive behind some seats. The laser tracked across the passenger area, cutting into tables and seats.

Ashtin threw an energy blade, and it sliced the weapon in half. The blaster hit the metal floor with a clunk.

Kennedy popped her head up. "Someone left us a gift."

He grunted and touched the console. The screen flickered. "Someone rerouted power away from the command console." He swiped, working to get the power back. They needed the ship's logs.

And the security feed.

The screen flickered, then died.

Come on. He gritted his teeth.

"Ashtin? I found something."

He turned and saw Kennedy holding something golden.

He sucked in a breath. It was an intricate gold twist.

Carys had been wearing it at the ball.

"That's Carys' earring," he gritted out.

Kennedy strode over to him. "Then we're on the right track. We're going to find her."

He nodded and turned back to the console. The lights started blinking. "The power is still fluctuating—"

Kennedy kicked the console. It flared to life. She smiled. "My dad used to say a swift kick could solve lots of problems."

Ashtin shook his head and started searching the ship's logs. "They definitely came from Oron. The internal camera feed has been wiped. There is external footage." He touched the screen.

The feed showed the exterior cavern, and a second ship flying out, its engine exhaust glowing orange.

"An Uruta cruiser." He scowled at the image. "It's much faster than this rusted freighter." *Gul.* They could be anywhere.

"Where are they headed?" She leaned over his shoulder. "Is there a record? Anything that gives us a clue?"

He swiped furiously. They couldn't have come this far only to lose Carys and Sten. "Wait, there's a star chart."

"And?" She leaned closer, brushing against him.

Ashtin had never liked being touched much, but he liked it when she touched him.

"There's a planet marked." He bit off a curse.

"Bad news?"

"The cruiser is headed for Kravaa III."

Kennedy's brows rose. "That doesn't mean anything to me."

"Kravaa III is a place the scum of the quadrant like to call home. It's just outside Oronis space. We keep an eye on it, but mostly we steer clear. It's overcrowded and riddled with pollution. It's full of black-market thieves, pirates, smugglers..."

"Sounds delightful."

He grunted.

"We need to check it out," she said.

Ashtin was silent. He didn't want to take Kennedy to

that *gul*-vexed cesspool, but he knew now that she could handle herself. The memory of her facing down the beast in the tunnel and the swamp monster hit him. Yes, Sub-Captain Kennedy Black could handle anything, it seemed.

Could she handle the growing desire inside him? His need for her?

She groaned. "So do we need to climb back through the tunnels?" She winced. "I'm sure our spiked friend would be happy to see us again."

"No."

She glanced at the cavern entrance. He noticed she hadn't gotten very close to the edge.

"I'm not jumping with you. Nope." She shook her head. "It's way too high."

He smiled. "I found something that gives Kennedy Black pause."

"Rub it in," she muttered.

He cleared his throat. "I dislike storms."

"What?" She blinked.

"Storms with thunder and lightning. I don't like them."

She cocked her head. "You, the deadly knightmaster, are afraid of storms?"

"I said I dislike them. I can operate in them, but I'd prefer not to."

Her lips quirked. "Thanks for sharing, but I'm still not jumping."

"We don't need to." He'd already activated their way out.

A second later, there was a roar of sound. Kennedy jolted.

His ship rose into view, flying on autopilot, and hovering at the cavern entrance.

Slowly, it flew in, and landed in front of them.

"Nice." She smiled.

The door opened and a metallic ball whizzed out. Beep zoomed straight for Kennedy, whizzing around her and beeping.

"I'm fine, Beep. We're both okay." She stroked the drone.

Ashtin narrowed his gaze. The drone appeared to... care for Kennedy. "What kind of experimental program did he belong to?"

She looked up. "Why?"

"Is he sentient?"

She pulled a face. "No. Maybe? No one knows for sure." Beep nuzzled her ear. "They were designed to assist officers. About a dozen of us were assigned drones, but the program didn't work out as Space Corps had hoped, and they shut it down. On the last day, Beep and I got electrocuted."

"What?" Ashtin demanded. "Were you hurt?" The idea that he might never have met her felt like a blow to the gut.

"No. A conduit on the ship we were on blew. I got a zap and was out for minute. Beep really got fried. He dropped to the ground, no lights, no power. I thought he was finished, then he powered up and went a little crazy." She smiled. "He was darting around like a drunken bee, and after that, he refused to leave me."

"And you understand him?"

She smiled. "Yes. We know each other pretty well by now. I can interpret most of his beeps and mannerisms."

Ashtin eyed the drone. Beep seemed to look back. "All right, well, let's get aboard."

As they settled on the ship, he watched her. He had to admit it. He already trusted her. There was no way this woman had betrayed him, or the Oronis.

He wanted her, more than he'd wanted anyone.

His gloved hand curled. He *had* to stay focused on his mission. On finding his queen and friend.

The entire Oronis were depending on him.

He couldn't let them down.

But for the first time in a long time, he had a partner at his side.

WELL, Ashtin hadn't lied. Kravaa III was rough, seedy... and also awesome.

Everywhere Kennedy looked, there was something interesting to look at, and she was busy trying to absorb it all.

The buildings were tall, spearing into the darkening sky. It was late afternoon, but the height of the buildings left the streets in shadow. Lights blinked and glowed and glittered everywhere. Neon-pink signs blinked over shops, blue-neon advertisements offered everything an unscrupulous shopper could want, and golden lanterns were strung across the streets. Garish awnings covered shop fronts, and high overhead, covered walkways spanned the air between buildings, and aerial transport zipped across the sky like migrating bats.

No stars shone in the murky sky. The pollution here was off the charts. Ashtin had given her a booster shot before they'd left the ship to help her lungs combat some of the air pollutants.

Poor Beep was missing out. Her drone had been very displeased to be once again confined to the ship at the nearby spaceport.

Ashtin was tense. She could feel it pumping off him. They were both wearing hooded robes. He'd wanted them to lay low and blend in.

They walked past a woman pulling a screaming child behind her. Two huge aliens of a species Kennedy didn't know crossed by them, their conversation consisting of grunts and growls. She could smell cooking meat. A man and a woman were manning portable grills on the footpath, yelling at each other in the good-natured way of old friends.

Her parents would've loved this place.

Kennedy breathed in. Beneath the roasting food, there was also the undertone of grit and decay. There were side alleys with no bright lights, and shadows moving in the darkness. Her senses were in danger of becoming overwhelmed.

She needed to focus on their mission. "So, who's this contact we're going to see?"

Ashtin scanned the street, then looked at her. "Boost. He's a broker. He buys and sells anything, but mostly information." Ashtin scowled. "He's about as trustworthy as a ravenous *dargor* beside a banquet table."

She made a mental note to look up a *dargor* later. "I'm guessing honorable knights don't like dealing with dishonorable scum."

"Correct." He sighed. "But finding Carys and Sten is more important. I'll do whatever needs to be done."

She touched his arm. "You're not doing it alone."

"I know." His voice was low, intimate.

She felt a shiver inside. God, it would be really dumb to fall for this Oronis knight. She would never, ever be the most important thing to him, always coming second to his duty. She pushed the thought away, turning her attention back to the multitude of sights around them.

"I wonder how Kaden and Nea are doing on the *Helios*?" she asked.

"I trust they'll do everything they can to follow that stealth trail."

"If they don't kill each other first. I got the impression they didn't like each other much."

"We all trained together as young knights. Those two always fought. Kaden loved to poke at Nea, and she invariably reacted." Ashtin glanced at her. "But they are both loyal and dedicated. They'll put their mission first."

The transport traffic thickened, and Kennedy focused on making sure she didn't get taken out by a speeding vehicle. The air smelled like exhaust fumes and left a chemical taste in her mouth.

They moved as quickly as they could through the crowded grid of streets. There were shops selling everything from clothing and weapons, to drugs and sex. Overhead, strings of lanterns bounced in the air, clothes fluttered on lines, and banners clogged the space above the street.

"The Festival of Lights is coming," he said. "Everyone decorates and celebrates."

"Celebrates what?"

"Nothing in particular. It's just an excuse to party."

A wiry man stepped out of an alley. He moved in front of Kennedy, and held some sort of chunky blaster in his hand.

"I want your weapons and valuables," he rasped.

She raised a brow. "You don't want to do this. Just walk away."

"Now!" He jerked the weapon.

She shook her head. "Really, you're making a huge mistake."

The man was sweating and shaking, clearly on some sort of drug, or otherwise impaired. "Give me what you've got!" Spittle flew from his mouth.

She sensed Ashtin readying to attack.

Kennedy kicked the man. The front kick sent him slamming into the wall of the nearby building.

"Look, I could take you down, and I think you'd prefer me doing it than him." She jerked her thumb at Ashtin.

He flicked his hood off, his face sharp, his blue eyes glowing.

Their would-be attacker made a choked sound.

"Or you could run," she suggested.

The man spun and took off, his feet slapping on the dirty pavement as he disappeared back into the alley.

"Well done," Ashtin said. "We want to keep a low

profile. The gangs here would love to get their hands on an Oronis knight."

"Why?"

"To dissect me for my combat implants."

Her heart kicked at her ribs. The image of that made everything in her revolt. "Okay, let's make sure we avoid that."

"This way." They finally stopped outside one of the many buildings. There was a small shop on the lower level selling electronics, but Ashtin pushed open a side door marked in an unfamiliar language.

A set of dingy stairs headed up, and somewhere she heard a baby wailing. The bright screens on the walls of the stairwell advertised all kinds of things. A few she was sure were X-rated.

Three floors up, they stopped at an unmarked door, and Ashtin knocked three times.

A small camera slid out of the wall, studied them for a beat, then the door opened.

Inside was nicer than outside. The open-plan apartment had large windows, with a view of the street. The polished floor looked like concrete, and there wasn't much furniture, but at the far end of the room sat three huge computer screens, and a man hunched in a seat that floated off the ground, and looked like half an egg.

"Boost." Ashtin strode across the room.

The seat turned. "Knightmaster Ashtin. Hope you've been smooth. It's been a long time, Knightman."

The man was thin, and wore huge goggles that made his dark eyes look enormous. His hair was a tangled cloud streaked in red and green.

"Not long enough," Ashtin said.

The man chuckled. "Come now, Kravaa III is so charming." The man's gaze flicked to Kennedy. He straightened in his seat. "What are you? You're not Oronis."

Ashtin pressed an arm across her chest. "She's with me."

Boost sniffed, clearly disappointed. "Fine. What do you need?"

"A ship arrived here over the last day. An Uruta cruiser carrying live cargo. I need to know where it landed, and where the cargo was taken."

"Lots of ships come and go. It'll take time." The man smiled. He had a gold tooth. "And it will cost you."

"I'll pay." Ashtin put his hands in his robes. "And an extra sum to keep my business quiet." He set several bronze, octagonal chips on the desk.

Boost eyed them, and nodded. "I'll be in touch. Go, enjoy the sights and pleasures of Kravaa III." He laughed like he'd made the funniest joke in the world.

Ashtin took Kennedy's arm, and led her out of the building.

"Nice friend you have," she said.

"He's not a friend, but he can be useful."

On the street, they paused for a moment, then Ashtin started down the sidewalk. Transports zoomed past.

"What now?" she asked.

"We wait. We'll find a place to eat."

Kennedy perked up. She wanted to try the food on this planet, questionable as it might be. She glanced around, her gaze landing on a man across the street, leaning against a neon sign and watching them.

The back of her neck prickled. She glanced back, as if she were looking at the transports. Two people appeared to be keeping pace behind them.

"We have company," she murmured.

"I know." Ashtin turned down an alley.

Adrenaline surged, and she hid a smile.

They'd only taken a few steps, when two large shadows stepped in front of them.

One man was humanoid, and not much taller than Kennedy. The other one was a huge, hulking giant with a bald head, bumpy, red skin, and reinforced knuckles.

Ambush.

The three men from the street blocked the alley behind them.

"Oh no," Kennedy dead-panned.

Internally, she was mad. These men had to be involved with framing Earth for Carys' abduction. Or they knew who was.

"Kill them," the giant rumbled.

Four of the men attacked.

CHAPTER TWELVE

Tossing his arms back, Ashtin threw off the hood and cloak.

Three attackers rushed at him, while the big alien hung back, the cowardly *gul*, and watched. He was clearly the one in charge. A fourth attacker charged at Kennedy.

They'd clearly decided he was the biggest threat.

He smiled. *Bad mistake.*

Ashtin threw his hands forward. An energy blade sliced out of his palm, cutting into the first man. The other two leaped, and Ashtin spun. He snapped a kick upward, and hit one in the chest. He whirled and grabbed the third man by the front of his shirt, and tossed him. He slammed into the wall.

Ashtin lifted his head.

Kennedy had her attacker on the ground, her boot pressed to his neck. The man was groaning.

Ashtin met her gaze. She smiled, then they both looked at the giant.

The alien was standing there, breathing heavily, shock on his ugly face.

"Who hired you?" Ashtin demanded.

The man grunted, then pulled out a large weapon. Ice flooded Ashtin's veins. It was an old blaster weapon that had been outlawed decades ago.

He ran and shoved Kennedy out of the way.

He heard the distinctive whirring sound, then a *thump*. The energy blast hit the wall behind them, and it disintegrated to dust.

Kennedy's mouth dropped open. "What the hell?"

"It's a disintegrator. One hit, and you're gone." He dragged her up.

Their assailant fired again.

The next blast hit an overflowing trash receptacle, which disappeared in a puff of smoke.

By the coward's bones. They needed to get away.

He had to get Kennedy out of there. He tossed an energy ball at the giant, and the man dove for cover.

"Go!" Holding Kennedy's hand, Ashtin sprinted deeper into the alley.

"Shit," she bit out.

It was a dead end.

Ashtin glanced around, and spotted a metal stairway attached to a nearby building.

"Up." He gripped her waist and tossed her into the air. She gripped the metal railing, and hauled herself upward.

The disintegrator whirred again. Ashtin ducked as the blast hit another wall. He bent his legs and jumped, using his implants to leap high. He gripped the metal of the stairway, and climbed.

There was a sharp whistle from below. He glanced down and spotted three smaller shapes at the giant's feet. The animals circled around the man's legs.

Zalga. Vicious, agile canines that could climb. They had small eyes, but a very good sense of smell. They also had sharp claws, and loved to tear up their prey.

"Hunt," the giant rumbled.

The three *zalgas* loped toward the building and started up the stone wall.

"Faster, Kennedy."

"What the hell are those?" she asked.

"*Zalgas.* Sharp claws, love to tear up their prey, excellent sense of smell."

"Freaking great." She hurried up the stairs, footsteps clanging on the metal.

Ashtin glanced over and saw a *zalga* clawing its way up the wall. One of them let out a wild howl.

He heard the disintegrator fire again. It hit the bottom of the metal stairs, and the entire staircase shook. He gripped the railing, and Kennedy did the same. He looked over.

He cursed. The bottom of the stairs was a melted, twisted wreck. Molten metal dripped down to the alley below.

"Faster," he said again.

"I'm going as fast as I can." But she picked up speed. He stayed right behind her.

Finally, they ran out onto the roof of the building. Cooling units and air recyclers dotted the area. Other buildings rose up around them. They sprinted across the rooftop. Some residents had set up chairs in one corner, a sad little spot, littered with empty drink containers.

They reached the other side. Down below, the space above the street was crisscrossed with lines of lanterns and decorations. Banners flapped in the breeze.

Ashtin looked down. "We'll—"

An excited howl cut him off.

The three *zalgas* climbed onto the roof.

They growled, their rangy bodies, covered in leathery skin, slinking across the ground.

Kennedy pulled out her blaster and fired. Ashtin formed his energy sword. His hand curled around the hilt.

One *zalga* went down under the laser fire. He sprinted toward another of the creatures. With a growl, one leaped at him, claws flashing.

He swung the sword and sliced the animal open. With a yelp, the *zalga* dropped to the ground, and Ashtin rolled.

He rose and spun. The final *zalga* was advancing on Kennedy.

With a single thought to his implant, the sword flowed into a whiplike ribbon of blue energy. It snapped taut and hit the *zalga*. Its leathery skin split, and it let out a howl. Injured, it darted back.

Kennedy opened fire. She didn't let up until the *zalga* collapsed and stopped moving.

He met Kennedy's gaze and smiled. She smiled back, lowering her weapon.

A door banged open.

Whirling, Ashtin saw the giant step out of a doorway. The man swiveled, and aimed the disintegrator straight at Ashtin.

Time slowed. He was already moving, but he knew the attacker's weapon would track him. The disintegrator beam would hit him dead on.

Kennedy yelled, her arms pumping as she sprinted.

Toward the giant.

No. By the coward's bones. No.

She leaped onto the giant's back.

The disintegrator flew from the man's hands. She'd hit him hard, and he staggered back, fighting her.

No. They were too close to the edge of the roof.

Suddenly, a metallic ball zoomed in from nowhere. It whizzed around the giant, ramming into the alien's head.

The man bellowed, one hand swatting at Beep while he tried to yank Kennedy off him.

The alien took an unsteady step. He was right at the edge of the roof.

No. Ashtin saw the man teeter.

"Kennedy!" Ashtin ran.

But it was too late. The giant lost his balance and held on tight to Kennedy.

The pair toppled over the edge of the building.

"*Kennedy!*" Ashtin yelled.

KENNEDY'S STOMACH DROPPED, then she was falling.

The giant alien growled, his legs thrashing.

She bent her legs and got her feet up, then kicked him in the gut. He let her go, one huge hand yanking on her hair before she was free.

She bounced off a line of lanterns, her body spinning wildly. *Shit.* She hit another line, then another. A banner hit her in the face.

Fuck. She didn't want to die.

She saw two lines strung close together and reached for them. She hit, and they tangled around her. Her body jerked, and the lines snapped taut.

She was yanked to a violent stop, hanging upside down, just meters above the dirty street.

She blew out a breath. *Thank God.*

Heart racing, she swallowed, and saw the giant hadn't been so lucky.

He'd hit the ground, his legs bent at awkward angles, and he was moaning softly.

Kennedy tried to move, but she was too tangled. She dragged in a breath.

A second later, she saw Ashtin leap down and land in a crouch in the middle of the street. He straightened, scanning frantically. He barely paid any attention to the injured giant. He spun, looked up, then spotted her.

Her lungs locked.

The feral look on his face made it hard for her to breathe. He strode over.

"Are you all right?" His voice was a deep rasp.

"Just hanging around."

He shot her a dark look.

"Sorry. Too soon to joke. I'm fine."

He cut her free, and a second later, she found herself in strong arms.

He went down on one knee, cradling her to his chest. He didn't pay any attention to the small crowd of onlookers who'd gathered, or the stopped transports. He pressed his face to the top of her head.

"When I saw you fall..." His strong body shuddered.

"Hey." Kennedy shifted and touched his cheek.

His blue eyes were ablaze.

"I thought you were dead," he said quietly.

"I'm not dead. I'm right here." She took his hand and pressed it to her chest, over her beating heart. "I'm very much alive."

He dragged in a deep breath. "Kennedy..."

She decided to stop questioning this never-ending pull that she felt toward this man, this alien knight.

She pressed her mouth to his.

He kissed her like he was trying to steal as much of her taste as he could. She felt his relief mingled with his desire, his tongue stroking and stroking. He groaned, dragged her closer, their bodies plastered together.

The need inside her was a huge, growing thing.

Her tongue stroked his, and she shifted, rubbing against him.

A series of frantic beeps interrupted.

She broke the kiss to see a frenzied Beep buzzing around. "I'm all right, Beep."

The drone burrowed against her hair, let out a beep.

"You're supposed to be on the ship," she said tartly.

Her drone ignored her. Then, after a small pause,

Beep flew over to Ashtin and gently bumped against his temple.

Ashtin looked surprised.

She smiled. "You must have grown on him."

Her knight pressed his forehead to hers. "We aren't safe here."

He was thinking about safety? Of course, he was. She managed a nod.

Another pained sound came from the giant. As Ashtin rose and set her on her feet, she looked at the alien and winced at his injuries.

There was no pity on Ashtin's face as he strode over to the man.

"Who sent you?"

The giant groaned.

"Who ordered you to kill us?" Ashtin's tone was slow and steady.

The giant sucked in a shaky breath. "Paid... To attack any Oronis knight that appeared on planet."

Ashtin crouched. "By who?"

Another shuddering breath. "Broker named Jaggex. Paid in solid Xerusian credits. Said it would just be one knight. Easy target."

Ashtin rose. "You made a mistake believing that. Where do I find this Jaggex?"

The giant's eyelids flickered. "Nightcrawler District."

Ashtin spun and took Kennedy's hand.

"Do we just leave him here?" she asked as Beep hovered over her left shoulder.

"Enforcement will pick him up eventually."

They strode to the end of the street, then turned left.

They came out at a large intersection. Transports whizzed past, and a droid was cleaning the street. A gang of teenagers loitered on one corner.

"Where's the Nightcrawler District?" she asked.

"Not far from here." He stalked into an alley, then pushed her against the wall, making her gasp.

He cupped her cheeks. "Are you sure you aren't hurt?"

"I'm sure, Ashtin." His eyes were still full of horrible shadows. "Later, when we're safe, I'll let you check."

Now, fire ignited in the depths of his blue eyes. His hands clenched on her arms. His mouth took hers—firm, hard, but unfortunately far too quick.

"Let's get to the Nightcrawler District and find this Jaggex, then I'll check in with Boost."

"Maybe this broker knows where Knightqueen Carys is," Kennedy said.

"We'll follow all the leads until we find her." Ashtin stepped back.

They walked back onto the street. Beep stayed close, but swiveled around and she knew he was recording. As they traveled farther, the streets became narrower, more trash littered the pavement, many of the buildings had broken windows, and the neon signs only half blinked on.

Ashtin stopped at a small restaurant on the street. It was just a large window, with a bench and four seats out on the pavement. Inside, large pots bubbled, and two workers moved back and forth.

While Ashtin spoke quietly to the restaurant owner, Kennedy scanned the street. She saw one alien man with four arms.

Wow. She itched to take a picture and find out what species he was.

Ashtin returned holding something in his hand. "Jaggex's building is one block down, on the corner. The man said we can't miss it." He held out a small, wrapped bundle.

Whatever it was, it smelled good. She unwrapped it to find some sort of bread with meat and sauce inside. "Do I want to know what this is?"

Ashtin took a bite of his and swallowed. "Probably not. But we need to refuel."

Kennedy tried the food. It didn't taste as good as it smelled, but it wasn't half bad, and she discovered she was starving.

Once she was done, the side of Beep's shell opened, and a small arm extended. He took the wrapper from her and raced away, dumping it in a trash receptacle, before zooming back.

She lifted her chin. "All right, let's go pay this Jaggex a visit."

CHAPTER THIRTEEN

Ashtin strode down the street, keeping his expression emotionless.

But inside, everything was still churning. Watching Kennedy fall off that building...

His gut cramped.

She's alive. His fingers tightened on hers. *Unharmed.* But he would check that fact for himself later. Maybe that would ease these terrible emotions.

For now, he'd do his duty, then he would get her safe.

He was realizing that taking care of Kennedy Black had become a part of his duty, too. One he was desperate to carry out.

He wanted to take care of her in every way possible.

They came to the end of the street, and he heard her make a sound.

"I think we found Jaggex," she said.

The building wasn't tall, but it was covered in various dishes and other communications technology. There wasn't any free space on the outside of the building.

"It looks like the place is a magnet and all this...stuff attached to it." She shook her head.

Ashtin frowned. "It's a mix of various alien technologies." He noted an Oronis-made receiver nestled among the others on the wall.

They found a doorway with a screen beside it. Ashtin waved Kennedy in front, then he stood to the side, out of view. Beep flew over and hovered by his shoulder.

She touched the screen.

"What?" a male voice barked.

"Hi, I need to buy something. I heard you can help me. I have credits."

"I'm busy."

"*A lot* of credits."

A pause. "Fine."

The door slid open. Ashtin nodded, and they headed up.

At the top of the landing, a wide door whispered open, and they walked into disarray.

Ashtin wrinkled his nose. The space was packed with gadgets and tech—computers, engine parts, entertainment devices, weapons. Everything was stacked haphazardly over shelves and tables. There were some things he didn't even recognize, and others he knew were from all over the quadrant.

"Welcome, welcome." A thin man appeared in the doorway. He had long, platinum hair pulled back in a tail, and moon-pale skin. One of his eyes was prosthetic, and Ashtin knew that particular model was so you could process data faster on a comp system.

Ashtin made sure he stayed out of the man's line of sight.

The broker threw his arms wide. "Whatever you need, Jaggex has it. That includes information."

"And you broker deals for people?" Kennedy asked.

"For the right price." Jaggex smiled, eyeing her. "Definitely for a pretty thing like you. I have whatever you need." He waved at the devices around him. "I'm a connoisseur. I collect exotic tech from across the galaxy. From planets without interstellar travel, even."

"Impressive," Kennedy replied.

Beep made a sound, sticking close to her.

The broker's attention zeroed in on the drone. "What's this?" His prosthetic eye zoomed in. "Hmm, I don't have one of those. I'll offer you a hundred Kravaa credits."

"He's not for sale," she said firmly.

"Two hundred."

Kennedy rested her hand on her holstered blaster. "No. Now, have you brokered any deals lately?"

Jaggex moved with the nervous jitter of someone who spent too much time plugged into information streams. Ashtin also saw he had a prosthetic hand. It was metallic, with built-in receptors on the fingertips for jacking into computer systems. He would have had his hand removed to have this one attached.

"I'm very good at what I do, so I've brokered lots of deals." Jaggex grinned. "Whatever you want, I'll make it happen."

Ashtin stepped into view.

The broker froze, his voice stuttering.

"How about organizing for an Oronis knight to be attacked?" Ashtin asked silkily.

"D-don't, don't kill me." Jaggex backed up and ran into a table laden with piles of gadgets. Several of them clattered to the floor.

Ashtin advanced. "Who did you broker the deal for?"

"I...I never give out my clients' names. In my line of work, it'll get you killed."

"Who?"

Jaggex swallowed, his cybernetic eye moving around like crazy. "I... I..."

"He's not happy, Jaggex," Kennedy said. "I've seen him fight. He's deadly. But you already know that just looking at him."

Ashtin heard admiration in her voice, and for a second, he was distracted from his target. Knowing she liked watching him fight made his cock tighten.

By the coward's bones. He fought for some control and glared at the broker.

"The Gek'Dragar!" Jaggex cried. "I was contacted by them. They threatened me. I just brokered the deal."

"Did they tell you anything else?" Ashtin demanded.

"No! *No.* They were very tightlipped." Jaggex swiped a shaking hand across his mouth. "I read between the lines. They're planning something big, and they don't want any Oronis knights to interfere."

From all the readings of the man's biosigns, he was telling the truth. This was another dead end.

"Hey, this is from Earth," Kennedy said.

Ashtin turned and saw her holding up a palm-sized device. It had a small, circular logo on it.

"So is this." She grabbed another gadget. She started pawing through the tech on the table.

"Be careful," Jaggex yelped. "All of that is unique. Valuable."

"This is off a Space Corps ship." She spun to the man. "Where did you get this?"

"I'm a collector."

"And a thief," Ashtin added.

Jaggex looked affronted. "I don't steal."

"But you buy stolen goods," Kennedy said.

"I acquire so many things—" he held his palms out "—there's no way to know if it's stolen or not."

"Who have you sold Earth tech to?" Ashtin demanded.

Jaggex looked nervous again. "Oh, well, I could check my records—"

"Answer my question," Ashtin snapped.

The man jolted "The Gek'Dragar. They specifically requested it and purchased several items."

"A tablet like this?" Kennedy held one up. It was nearly identical to the one they'd found on Oron.

Jaggex nodded vigorously.

Ashtin met her gaze. The Gek'Dragar had set Earth up. Just as she'd told him. To muddy the situation and put them at odds.

But Kennedy hadn't allowed it. She'd stayed strong, and stuck to her convictions.

He narrowed his gaze on the broker. "If I ever have to return here—"

"You won't." Jaggex held up his hands. "I won't broker *any* more deals with the Gek'Dragar. I promise."

Beep let out an unhappy chirp.

Yes, Ashtin didn't believe it either. With one last glare for the broker, he nodded at Kennedy, and they swept out.

BACK ON THE STREET, Kennedy felt a little lighter, as though a large weight had been lifted.

She'd proven the Earth was *not* involved with the Gek'Dragar.

She realized now it didn't matter as much as she'd expected. Not when she already knew that Ashtin believed her.

She eyed him. God, he was handsome. But he was also tense, his jaw tight.

She knew he was worried. They still had no idea where the knightqueen and her guard were.

"What next?" she asked.

"I'll contact Boost and see if he's found the ship."

She stood against the wall of the building while Ashtin spoke quietly into his communicator. She watched the street, seeing two little girls skipping on the pavement, a companion droid sticking close by.

She smiled. They could be little girls from Earth. "Beep, can you get a shot of those girls?"

Beep swiveled and his lights flashed. She knew he'd taken a picture of the girls from the back, catching one little girl mid skip while the other little girl reached for the droid's hand.

"Kennedy?"

She looked at Ashtin. "Any news?"

He gave her a frustrated look. "No, but Boost says he's narrowed the search down. He should have something for us by morning."

"Okay." She ran a hand through her hair. She hated having to wait.

"We need food and rest." He paused. "And I need to check you for injuries."

Her pulse jumped.

"There's an Oronis safe house not far from here." He held out a hand.

She put hers in his.

They hadn't gone far when he stopped at a large, glass structure. They stepped into an elevator that whisked them up two levels. When the glass doors parted, they stepped out onto a long platform that had a small, aerial transport pulling away at the far end.

"We'll get a transport to the safe house," he told her.

They walked to the end of the platform, and watched another of the transports pull in. They were clearly automated, with no driver. The top of the transport was made of glass.

It pulled to a stop and the top part slid open.

He pulled her inside. There were two bench seats on either side and he pulled her down to sit on one. As Beep flew in, the glass roof closed.

Ashtin touched a screen, then inputted their destination and payment details. The transport pulled away smoothly.

The vehicle did a turn and picked up speed, flying between two buildings.

"So amazing." Kennedy watched the city. It was a blur of different colors. Night had fallen, and the light pollution was a bright glow below.

The transport rose, the buildings got higher and higher.

"This planet is fascinating, but there aren't enough trees or plant life," she said.

"Agreed. That contributes to their pollution problem."

He stroked a hand down her back, and instantly she wasn't interested in the city anymore.

His gaze was unwavering, locked on her. "There'll be food and clean clothes at the safe house."

She moaned. "Wonderful." She really wanted a shower.

Plus, she and this fascinating, attractive man would be alone for the night. Her blood heated.

"And I have to check you for injuries," Ashtin's voice lowered.

"You know I'm not hurt."

His hands moved to her shoulders. "I can't get the picture of you falling off that building out of my head, Kennedy. I need to check, to wash that image away, and how it made me feel."

Desire rose up, coiling in her belly. She'd never felt like this before. Never wanted a man this much before. "How did it make you feel?"

"Terrified. I'm a knight. Fear isn't something I'm supposed to feel."

She shifted closer to him, tracing her fingers over his face, his strong jaw.

"*Kennedy.*" A low whisper.

She pressed her lips to his.

Instantly, strong arms yanked her in. The kiss was deep, desperate, and need exploded inside her.

God, she was so hungry for him. It was like she needed him to survive.

She moaned, pressing into him. He dragged her close and she straddled his lap.

He slid a hand into her hair. "Kennedy, I want to take care of you."

"You are."

He bit her lip, groaned. "I'm letting my own needs take over."

She kissed his jaw. "I need you to feel good, too."

She looked at his face. His pupils were wide, his pulse beating fast on the side of his neck. Hunger throbbed off him.

Same as the hunger inside her.

She shifted on his lap, grinding down. His erection was a solid bar beneath her. His hands clamped on her hips.

Kennedy rolled her hips and he groaned, pulling her closer.

"Kiss me, Knightmaster Ashtin. That's an order."

He made a deep, masculine sound, then his mouth was on hers.

Oh. *God.*

His lips were hard on hers, and the kiss had a wild edge. His tongue licked hers, his head angling so he could kiss her deeper. The thick cock beneath her was getting harder. She undulated, moaning, her fingers spearing into his thick hair.

Suddenly, the transport pulled to a stop.

Ashtin's hands gripped her hips and clenched. Kennedy raised her head, blinking to clear the haze of desire.

Beep was watching them, motionless.

Ashtin cleared his throat. "We've arrived at the safe house."

"Right." It almost hurt to climb off him.

He took her hand, and her fingers tingled. He pulled her out of the transport.

"Beep, come on," she said.

The wind tugged at her hair. They were very high up. The air was cleaner up here, with none of the ugly, rotting street smells. She breathed deeply.

"Wow, we're so high." They stood on a platform hanging off the side of one of the tallest buildings.

As the aerial transport pulled away soundlessly, she looked down at the city below. It looked like a painting.

Just wow. Incredible.

Then she swiveled and took in Ashtin. His hair ruffled by the breeze.

He pulled her toward the penthouse. Of course, the Oronis safe house was perched on top of a tall building. It was a sleek structure, with straight lines, but the walls were stained—she guessed from toxic rain—and the glass windows looked grimy. She couldn't see inside.

It was nothing like the beautiful architecture on Oron.

Oh well, she knew it would be safe, at least.

He pressed his palm to a scanner. "It tests for Oronis genetic material. It's the only way to get in."

The doors opened, and they stepped inside.

"Welcome Knightmaster Ashtin," a low computer voice intoned.

Kennedy sucked in a breath. "This is beautiful."

The inside of the penthouse was *nothing* like the outside. The Oronis had concealed a little hideaway on Kravaa III.

It gave her the same feel of the inside of Castle Aravena. It was open, with lots of gleaming, white-gray stone. As they walked in, they passed several small trees growing up through the floor.

The entry opened into a long living area with one wall made entirely of glass.

"The coating on the windows makes it impossible for anyone to see in," he told her. "But we can see out."

"It's like we're on top of the world," she murmured.

Comfortable, sleek furniture in stark white sat in the space, and the glass doors opened onto a wide terrace that was dominated by a large pool of glowing blue-purple water.

"Oh, my God." She strode to the glass, fingertips touching it. "The pool extends *off* the side of the building."

Ashtin smiled at her. "It does. There is also a clear dome over the terrace. No one can see the pool."

That smile. Her belly clenched almost painfully. She wanted him so damn much.

They'd probably only have this time together.

That wasn't a pleasant thought.

No. She wasn't thinking of the future right now. Only the present.

"Beep, lay low."

Her drone beeped at her.

"See if you can find somewhere to plug in and recharge for the night."

Another short beep, and the drone whizzed away, disappearing into the next room.

Kennedy started to unfasten her suit. It parted down the middle.

Ashtin stiffened. "What are you doing?" His voice came out sounding strangled.

She smiled. "I'm going for a swim in the pool." She shoved the rest of her clothes off, standing there naked.

Then she sauntered toward the terrace. The glass parted for her. She glanced back at her knight, who was as still as a statue, his gaze glued to her naked form.

Then she walked outside and into the warm water.

CHAPTER FOURTEEN

He couldn't drag his gaze off her.

Kennedy's body was every fantasy Ashtin had ever had in the dark of night. She was curvier than most Oronis women and he wanted to explore every curve. Hunger tore through him—strong, potent, wild.

No one had ever described him—cool, controlled Knightmaster Ashtin—as wild. But Kennedy brought it out in him.

He watched the water lap around her. The way he wanted to touch her.

Possess her.

As a knight, he was driven to serve. He'd never wanted things for himself.

But he wanted this woman from Earth.

He strode outside, tugging at his clothes. He stripped off his coat and shirt.

She turned in the pool, leaning against the far edge, hanging out over the long, dizzying drop. She didn't look at the view. No, she looked at him, her gaze running hungrily over his bare chest.

Ashtin kicked off the rest of his clothes and stepped into the water.

She floated there, watching him come toward her.

"Your skin should be pale from being on a ship so much," he said.

Her skin wasn't pale. It was a lovely golden color.

"I make sure I do time in the sunlight generator." She gazed at his chest. "You're much more bronze than me." She ran her tongue over her lips.

His cock felt heavy, full. Throbbing. His skin felt stretched taut over his body, and he smelled her scent.

"I'll check you over now." His voice was guttural.

She smiled, then gave a quick shake of her head. "Still all Mr. Overprotective."

"That's Knightmaster Overprotective." He wouldn't apologize for his need to keep her safe.

He took her arm and ran his hand up it. He heard her breath hitch. He touched her other arm, and checked it too.

She shivered. His gaze ran over her smooth shoulders. Her skin was like the finest Oronis silk. The tops of her firm breasts bobbed in the water, and he groaned.

She pressed into him, her mouth claiming his. Her breasts pressed against his bare chest. She slid a hand into his hair, kissing him back eagerly, her tongue dancing with his.

When her fingers moved lower, they bushed over the combat implants at the base of his neck. She stilled, and stroked them. "I want to see these."

"Later. I haven't finished checking you."

"So check." There was a hot, flirty look in her eyes.

He held her closer and moved toward the wide steps at the end of the pool. He sat and pulled her naked body onto his lap. He ran a hand up her back, then around her belly. He felt her draw in a breath.

"Does anywhere hurt?" he asked.

"Maybe."

"Where?"

She licked her lips and moved his palm to her breast.

He kneaded the soft flesh and she arched into him with a gasp. He found one nipple, tugged on it, and watched it harden.

"*Ashtin.*"

He lowered his head to the other breast and sucked on the nipple. She made an inarticulate sound.

He kept sucking, loving the way she moved. Loving the needy, desperate sounds she made. She didn't hide her desire, and he could smell her arousal, see the flush on her wet skin.

"Does it hurt anywhere else?"

She licked her lips again. "Yes, between my legs."

He ran one hand down her sleek thigh and pushed her legs apart. There was a tiny strip of dark hair above her sex. He spread her with his fingers, then stroked.

She jerked on a low moan, water splashing. "God, yes. *Please*, Ashtin."

She needed him. Needed what only he could give her. He stroked her soft flesh, his knuckle hitting a small, swollen nub. There were so many similarities between

163

her and the Oronis. It was clear Earth, Eon, and the Oronis came from a similar ancient ancestor.

"Do you want me to suck this?" he murmured.

She jerked. "Yes. God, yes."

"Do you want me to put my mouth here? To finally taste you?"

"*Ashtin.*" The word was almost a growl.

He spun and sat her on the uppermost step, her body out of the water.

He moved between her legs, spreading them wide. He blew over her needy flesh and she made a choked sound. He licked her, savoring her cry of pleasure. He absorbed her scent, her honey taste.

"You're...good at this," she panted.

He tongued that little nub, watching her every move to gauge what she liked most. "I'm a man who gives his all to his duty."

Her gaze met his. That cloudy gray he liked so much.

"Duty?"

"Yes, it's my duty to pleasure you." He sucked, holding her as she writhed. Her body shook, her thighs squeezing him.

Ashtin kept his mouth pleasuring her as he rubbed a finger across her slick flesh. He slid a finger inside her.

As her hips lifted, water splashed. He worked another finger inside her, sucking harder.

"Ashtin," she moaned.

Her body shook. He held her as she shuddered through her release. Suddenly he knew he could watch her like this, day after day.

She leaned back, panting. Then she lifted her head, her eyes blazing. "I need you inside me, Knightmaster."

His stomach clenched, his cock painful, his need so strong.

"As you desire." He scooped her up and walked out of the pool. Her arms and legs wrapped around him.

Her mouth met his hungrily as he strode inside.

KENNEDY PAID no attention to the décor as Ashtin carried her through the penthouse.

She was too busy kissing him, her body still humming from her orgasm. She needed him inside her so badly. She was throbbing.

But she also wanted to see him lose it, to give him pleasure.

Then he was laying her on a wide bed in a shadowed room. A glass ceiling arched overhead.

He knelt beside her, his gaze running over her naked, damp body.

There was a reverence there that made her throat tighten. No one had ever looked at her like that before.

She'd never been important enough to anybody.

Her gaze skated over his lean musculature, and stopped at his erect cock. It was long, rising up against his muscled abdomen.

Her thighs clenched, and she felt a rush of dampness between her legs.

He leaned over her and ran a possessive hand down her body, between her breasts and over her belly.

"What do you need now?" he asked her.

She felt a jolt of desire. She loved the way he was so focused on her, on giving her what she wanted.

What she needed.

"I want you inside me," she panted. She sent up a silent thank you for her Space Corps contraceptive implant.

His hand moved between her legs. "You want me here?" He thrust two fingers inside her.

She clenched on him. "*Yes.*"

"Do you know how many times I've imagined this?" His eyes glowed. "Imagined sliding inside you?"

She moaned.

"It started the first moment I met you, Kennedy."

God. "Inside me, Ashtin. *Now.*"

He pushed her legs apart and leaned over her. He rubbed the head of his cock against her.

She cried out. Her legs shifted, and she tucked them up tight against his sides. She saw the instant he lost the grip on his control.

With a low groan, he lodged the head of his cock inside her, then slammed home.

"*Ashtin.*"

He froze. "Did I hurt you?"

She shook her head, trying to get the words out. "No. You're thick."

She saw his faint smile. "And you're tight, but I think we fit just right."

She clamped her hands on his muscular ass. "*Move.*"

He rocked against her.

The haze of desire fogged her thoughts. He felt so good, so right.

He picked up the pace, thrusting inside her with strong, pumping movements.

She gripped his shoulders, holding on as the speed and depth of his wild strokes increased. She felt another release building—fast and hard.

"I want to watch you come with my cock inside you," he growled.

She pressed her head back into the pillow. "I want to feel you come inside me."

He made a deep, masculine sound.

Their eyes locked. She saw the desire on his face. Felt the way they were connected.

Her climax hit.

Crying out, she arched and felt him thrust deep, his cock deeply embedded inside her. As her inner muscles contracted, she heard his guttural groan, and felt him coming inside her.

Pleasure hit in long, undulating waves.

Kennedy felt boneless, her chest heaving.

He dropped down on her, their bodies still damp. She smiled. His hair was mussed and his cheekbones flushed with color. She liked seeing the always-in-control knightmaster a little messed up, for her.

She ruffled a hand through his thick hair. She felt... awesome. Her body was tingling. Sex had never been like this before.

It had usually been fun, and she'd thought satisfying, but this was like a possession. Her orgasms had blown her mind.

That's when she realized he was still hard inside her. "Ashtin?"

He'd come. She felt the wetness between her legs.

"Once isn't enough," he said, voice low.

"*Oh.*" Her belly fluttered.

He pulled out of her, and she bit her lip. She felt a terrible sense of emptiness, but then he flipped her over on her belly. He ran a hand down her spine, and cupped one ass cheek.

"It's going to be harder and faster now, Kennedy." He bent over her and bit the back of her neck. She squirmed.

He pushed her legs open, then before she could brace, slammed into her so fast, she cried out.

He slowly pulled out and thrust back in.

"Hold on, Kennedy."

She groped around and found the smooth, metal headboard. She gripped it as he started to move.

She moaned. Each thrust pushed her into the bed. She glanced back at him, and gasped.

He looked dangerous. His face was harsh, mouth a flat line, sharp arousal on his face.

And his eyes glinted with focused intensity.

He planted his fists in the bed either side of her, his muscles flexing as he moved inside her.

There was no control now. She was at his mercy.

But she knew this man, this fierce alien knight, would never hurt her.

Kennedy gripped the headboard harder, and gave herself up to the pleasure.

CHAPTER FIFTEEN

Ashtin carried a plate of high-nutrient food, and two nutrient-rich drinks, to the bedroom.

It was still early, and the sun hadn't risen yet, but he'd woken up ravenous.

He paused in the doorway, and just stared at her.

Kennedy lay sprawled on her stomach on the bed, sleeping deeply.

He'd used her hard, mercilessly, for hours. He hadn't been able to get enough of her.

And she hadn't just taken it, she'd reveled in it. She'd eagerly partaken in their intense lovemaking.

He had been driven to give her as much pleasure as he could. She'd climaxed so many times, her body a dream under his.

He'd also come many times within the tight clasp of her body. He'd kept going until they were both sweaty and exhausted. Finally, they'd slept for a few hours, his cock still inside her, her face pressed to his chest, and his hand tangled in her hair.

Ashtin had finally taken something for himself. Done exactly what he wanted.

Being so close to her, connected to her, made him realize how good it felt. To have someone be *his*.

His gaze lingered on her bare back. He was half hard again just looking at her, but he was determined now to look after her in other ways. To serve all her needs. She needed food and sustenance.

He realized with a jolt that he hadn't thought of Carys and Sten for the last few hours. He averted his gaze and stared at the floor. He couldn't forget that their lives were at stake. They were depending on him.

Until Boost contacted him, there was nothing he could do. For now, he could focus on Kennedy.

He walked to the well-rumpled bed and set the plate and glasses on the side table. Her hair was loose, and his fingers itched to touch those rich, brown strands. He knew how soft they were.

He ran a hand down her back, and she made a cute sound. He smiled, and lay down on his back beside her, stroking her skin.

She made another sound, and opened one eye. When she saw him, that eye widened.

"Oh, boy." Her voice was husky. "It wasn't just a really wild, amazing dream."

His lips twitched. "No."

As she shook sleep off, her gaze ran down his body, warmth seeping into her gray eyes.

"Food." He reached for the plate and grabbed a small item. He pressed it to her lips.

"It's a green cube," she said dubiously.

"It tastes good, I promise. It's packed full of nutrients."

She chewed, swallowed, and raised her brows. "It's not bad."

"Most food here on Kravaa III is highly processed, but full of vitamins and minerals."

They ate and drank. Ashtin didn't stop to think about how much he liked feeding her like this.

Caring for her.

Kennedy sat up, finishing her drink, but his gaze went straight to her breasts.

His cock began tenting the sheet. Those pebbled, pink nipples on top of the sweet curves of her breasts teased him. He saw a few bruises on her skin, and knew they'd come from his fingers, but he couldn't find it in him to feel too sorry.

She eyed him, smiling. She set her glass down, reaching over him, her breasts brushing his chest.

He sucked in a breath.

"Any word from your informant?" she asked.

"Not yet. Boost is not an early riser. It'll likely be a few more hours."

She made a humming sound, then straddled him. She shoved the sheet out of her way. Her knees pressed tight to his sides, and the already slick folds of her sex were rubbing along his cock. She ran her hands up his chest.

"I love your body, Ashtin."

"I love yours, too."

"*Mmm.*" She rocked against him. "I like it right here."

"I like it better when my hard cock is inside you."

"Soon, my Galahad. Now, turn over."

He cocked a brow at her order.

"I want to see your implants."

She'd touched them during the night, but hadn't had a chance to explore them up close.

Ashtin rolled onto his stomach.

She made a curious sound, and he felt the brief caress of her hand on his ass before her fingers dragged up his spine.

She touched each one of the black, metallic implants embedded along his spine.

"Fascinating."

He smiled against the sheet. She had that curious tone he recognized now, when she was lost in absorbing new things.

As her fingers caressed him, he shivered.

"Are they sensitive?" she asked.

"No." But any time she touched him, he felt it.

She touched the larger *oralite* implant at the back of his neck. She leaned closer and he felt the brush of her lips.

"You're pretty special, Knightmaster. What you can do with these is incredible."

"Every knight has them."

"Ah, but you all still have to train to use them, right?"

He rolled back over. "Yes."

She knelt there, naked and smiling, and his heart squeezed.

Then her gaze slid down his body and locked on his swollen cock. "Hmm, something else you have is pretty special."

She fisted his cock, stroked it.

With a groan, he pushed up into her fist. "Kennedy." When he started to sit up, she pushed him back down.

"Nuh-ah. It's my turn to explore you." Her thumb ran over the weeping tip of his cock. "To give you what you want. To make you feel good." Then she lowered her head.

When she licked along his length, he groaned, one hand clenching in the bed covers. The other slid into the silky strands of her brown hair.

"You're perfect," he growled.

She smiled at him, then opened her mouth and sucked him deep.

Desire twisted inside him. He sank into her sweet, warm mouth. She made a humming sound, her tongue exploring the ridges of him, and he groaned.

"So good, Kennedy." His voice was pure grit.

She sat up, licking her lips. There was pure fire in her eyes, need stamped all over her face. "Need you inside me."

She straddled him again. He ran his hands up her sides, cupped her breasts. She arched into him and made a hungry sound. Then she shifted her hips, settling against his throbbing cock. He could feel how wet she was.

A film of sweat slicked across Ashtin's skin, need like a supernova building inside him. He thought their night together would've lessened this wild desire.

It had only made it worse.

"*Kennedy.*"

Her palms clenched on his chest, and she lowered down, taking his cock inside her, bit by bit.

His hands fisted on the bed, and he groaned.

"It's nice having a big, powerful knight at my mercy," she murmured.

"I'm yours. Whatever you want or need, I'm yours."

A flash of emotion crossed her face. He thrust his hips up and she gasped. She was impaled on him, his cock lodged deep.

Then she started to move. She picked up her pace, hips rising and falling.

"Kennedy." He clasped her ass, urging her on.

"It's never been like this, Ashtin. So much. *So good.*"

He reared up and kissed her, his hands moving her faster on his cock. He reached down and rubbed that little nub he now knew so well.

A moment later, she screamed. Her body clenched tight, and her gaze locked with his.

Her release triggered his. Her body milked him, and he felt pleasure like a hot blade down his spine.

After a few moments, they still sat there, pressed together, Kennedy trembling against him.

"Every time gets better," she whispered.

He pulled her down to his chest and they lay sprawled together, feeling boneless and relaxed. He loved the way she nestled against him.

But something pricked at his contentment.

He was an Oronis knight. He couldn't let anyone become more important to him than his duty. His people and his queen were his sole focus. They had been for his entire life. His arms tightened on Kennedy.

Then he heard his communicator implant chime.

He reached up and touched his ear, as Kennedy lifted her head.

He read the incoming message.

"Boost has something for us."

She straightened. "Time to go."

KENNEDY FOLLOWED Ashtin back into Boost's apartment. Her skin still tingled, and she felt a few interesting twinges and aches.

She smiled to herself. She had zero regrets.

Every minute of the night had been amazing.

But she was afraid her feelings for him were growing way beyond her control.

She swallowed. There was no time to focus on that right now, but a part of her already knew how this would end.

Ashtin was an Oronis knight. Duty was his core, the air he breathed.

She was just an ordinary woman from Earth. She would never be the most important thing in his universe.

They'd enjoy each other, complete their mission, and then he'd go back to being the dedicated knight.

And she'd go home.

The pain in her chest was a sharp shock.

She had her work with Space Corps. It was enough. It had always been before.

She reached down and touched the holster where Beep was safely stowed. She felt her drone vibrate, like he could pick up her unsettled emotions.

"Boost," Ashtin barked.

The man raised a hand from his floating chair, his gaze glued to his screens.

"Yo, Knightman. You keeping smooth?"

Ashtin ignored the question. "You found the ship."

Boost spun his chair. "Sort of."

Ashtin made a low sound. "Don't joke about this. It's important."

Boost's brow creased and he readjusted his goggles. "You never did say what exactly was on that ship that is so important to you."

Kennedy felt anger building in her knight. She brushed his back with her fingers.

He paused and heaved in a breath. "Where is the ship?"

Boost's chair floated closer. "It was hard to find. They hid their tracks well, but not well enough for Boost. It landed at a small, private spaceport in Acrona. Right at the edge of the city."

"Thank you." Ashtin started to leave.

"Wait," the man cried. "It's not there anymore."

"What?" Ashtin spun.

Dammit. Kennedy's pulse jumped.

"The ship refueled and took off again. Twelve hours ago."

Ashtin cursed.

"No cargo was offloaded," Boost added. "I checked all the feeds for you." He sucked on a tooth. "For a bonus, I'll tell you where it's headed."

Ashtin stilled. "You know its destination?"

"I hacked its nav computer records. It did a dump as

it pulled out. It was headed to the Gammis quadrant. No idea why, because there's nothing out there but an asteroid field."

Kennedy noted a quick flash on Ashtin's face before he hid it.

"Payment will be transferred to your account," Ashtin said.

Boost lifted a hand. "See you next time, Knightman. I prefer working with you over Kaden. That dude is scary."

Kennedy followed Ashtin out. "This asteroid field means something to you?"

They reached the street level. His jaw worked. "Yes."

"Are you going to share?"

He stared blindly at the traffic.

She touched his arm. "Ashtin?"

He pulled her close, and pressed a kiss to her lips. It took her by surprise, and he looked a little shocked he'd done it. She knew he was a man who didn't commit public displays of affection.

"The asteroid field comes from the destroyed planet of Gammis. There's still a moon there—Gammis III. The field and the moon now orbit the system's sun. It was the location of the violent battle between the Oronis knights and the Gek'Dragar centuries ago."

"Oh, boy."

He nodded. "The planet was uninhabitable. It was destroyed in the fight. The moon is inhabitable, and held an old Oronis outpost. It was where the battle of Gammis III occurred. The final defeat of the Gek'Dragar."

Kennedy sucked in a breath. "And now the Gek'-

Dragar have abducted the knightqueen and taken her there."

"Yes. The outpost was called Castle Ishta. They must be going there to exact revenge."

She gripped his forearm. "We need to get there. Now."

"Kennedy, it's very dangerous. During the battle of Gammis III, the Gek'Dragar used fierce creatures in the fight."

"Like the *dirlox*?"

"Worse. Much larger, winged creatures, the size of a shuttle, with heavily scaled skin. They're extremely aggressive and live in space."

"They sound like dragons. From legends on Earth."

"They're called *draarkil*. Some escaped in the battle, and they've bred in the asteroid field. The *draarkil* attack anyone who approaches Gammis III. They can also emit a dangerous electrical charge."

"Wonderful." She ran a hand over her hair. "Electricity spitting dragons."

"It will be dangerous to get past them, but I must get to Castle Ishta and save Carys and Sten."

"*We*, Ashtin. We have to get there."

He gripped her hips. "You've done your bit. You proved Earth was not involved, you helped me find Carys and Sten's location."

"I'm coming."

"I don't want you to come."

Her heart contracted. She lifted her chin. "I can handle this. I've proved it."

His fingers tightened, and he pressed his forehead to hers. "It's not that."

"What is it?"

"I don't want you in danger. I don't want you to get hurt."

Her heart clenched, softened. "And I won't let you go alone. We're a team."

He pulled in a deep breath.

She went up on her toes and kissed his cheek, then the other, then pressed her mouth to his.

"A team," he murmured.

"Yes. Let's go and find your queen."

CHAPTER SIXTEEN

Gaze on the viewscreen, Ashtin watched as the first asteroids came into view. The console beeped, showing the size and makeup of the huge rocks.

"Jesus." Kennedy leaned forward, her gaze riveted to the screen. "The field is so dense."

In front of them, the asteroids whirled and moved, the smaller ones whizzing by fast.

Beep whizzed by, chirping loudly.

"It'll be fine, Beep," she said. "Chill."

"We can't fly through it," he said. "Our ship isn't large enough, and it doesn't have the shielding or weapons needed." He pointed. "There's the moon. Gammis III." It was just visible through the field of rocks. A small moon covered in bands of green and brown.

"How the hell do we get there, if our ship can't withstand hits from those asteroids?" she asked.

"We go in using exo-suits."

She blinked. "Exo-suits? You mean we *fly* through the asteroid field with only suits for protection?"

"Yes. We'll be more maneuverable."

"That's *crazy*."

"We can do it." He turned the ship and aimed for one of the large asteroids at the edge of the field. "We'll leave the ship there. On that asteroid. Then we'll suit up and fly out."

Kennedy scraped a hand through her hair, and gave a small laugh. "I didn't peg you for a risk taker, Galahad."

"I'm not. But I weigh the risks and assess the odds. And I'll take a calculated risk."

"All right. I trust you."

His head snapped up. Hearing her say that hit him right in the chest.

Kennedy trusted him.

And he was just realizing how much he trusted her. How much he would do for her.

He'd fight for her.

He'd kill for her.

He'd lay his life down for her.

This woman from Earth had earned his respect. She was smart, capable, courageous.

A true partner.

And she saw *him*, not just the dedicated knightmaster.

Ashtin turned his attention to the viewscreen. He had to stay focused to get this mission completed and keep her safe. He flew them toward the large asteroid.

It was made of a dark-brown rock, and craggy. It loomed above the ship, filling the viewscreen.

"What about the *draarkil*?" Kennedy asked.

"Nothing showing on scans. They live in tunnels that

181

they've carved into the asteroids. I'm guessing they haven't detected us yet."

But they would. Unless he and Kennedy could sneak in undetected, which was highly unlikely. He knew that the *draarkil* had extremely sensitive senses.

"The adult *draarkil* prefer space," he told her. "If we can avoid them, they should leave us alone on the moon."

"Sounds like a breeze."

He grabbed her hand. "Kennedy—"

She curled her fingers in his. "We can do this. Together."

He nodded and made himself focus on the controls. He flew to the asteroid and initiated the landing thrusters. The ship touched down with a dull thud, and he engaged the geo-locks. Hooks stabbed into the asteroid to secure the ship to the rock.

He rose. "Let's get suited up."

He opened lockers at the back of the ship and pulled out the long, silver spine of one of the exo-suits.

"It looks like a metallic backbone," Kennedy said.

"That's exactly what it is. Turn around."

She did and he pressed the device to her back. The spine adjusted to her size, then extended to clamp around the base of her neck.

"Activate it when you're ready," he said.

"All right." She stepped back and held her arms out.

The exo-suit activated. Silver bands of armor snapped around from the spine wrapping around her body.

He watched the metal cover her from head to toe, until only her face was left uncovered.

"Oh, wow," she said. "It actually looks like a suit of armor."

"Don't extend the wings until we're outside the ship." He turned and slipped on the spine of his exo-suit. The armor clamped into place on his body.

Beep appeared, doing a few circles around them.

"How do I look, Beep?" She posed for her drone. "Take a few pictures." When the drone butted against her chest, she sighed. "You can't come, buddy."

A low, long beep.

"It's too dangerous." She held out her palm and the drone nestled there. "Take care of the ship, okay. I'll see you when I get back."

Beep made a sound, then flew to Ashtin. He held his palm up and the drone sat on his hand. "I'll take care of her. I promise."

With another loud beep, the drone rose up into the air, watching them.

"Ready?" Ashtin asked her.

She nodded. "Let's do this."

They moved to the small airlock by the back door of the ship.

"Kennedy?"

"I know." She rose up and kissed him.

With a groan, he pulled her as close as he could, and kissed her back.

"We've got this." She winked at him.

He'd be with her every step of the way, whatever happened, whatever they faced.

He'd do whatever he had to in order to keep her safe.

"Close your helmet," he ordered.

Their visors snapped into place.

Ashtin pressed the control panel beside the door. A low warning chime sounded, then the outer door opened.

He jumped off the ship. He hung in space, then activated the suit's wings. They slid out either side of his body.

"Holy hell, that is so amazing," Kennedy said through the comm unit in the helmets.

"Let's get to that moon," he said.

"I'm right beside you, Knightmaster."

He liked her there, by his side.

He realized just how badly he wanted it. How important this woman was becoming to him.

Their propulsion systems activated, and they zoomed forward, deeper into the asteroid field.

It was time to find Knightqueen Carys, and stop the Gek'Dragar.

***

KENNEDY FLEW FAST and fought back a laugh.

She *loved* this suit.

She eyed Ashtin as they moved deeper into the asteroid belt. He flew with a power and grace that stole her breath away. The silver metal of the suit gleamed, and she could easily imagine him as a knight of old, in his armor, riding his steed into battle.

"Okay, the asteroid density is increasing." His deep voice echoed inside her helmet. "Switch to auto flight mode. The sensors in your suit will fly you out of the path of any debris."

"Switching now." The display on her visor flickered, highlighting and assessing the asteroids—location, density, geological makeup.

Then without any input from her, the suit turned her out of the path of a small asteroid. Her heart raced. It was exhilarating.

A large one rose up into view. Her suit tipped her sideways. She saw Ashtin's suit do the same. They dived, soaring past the asteroid. They were close enough that she could reach out and touch the rocky surface.

She laughed. She knew this was a serious, dangerous situation, but at the same time, it was an incredible experience.

Every part of this adventure had been amazing. Her gaze fell on the man beside her. Especially Ashtin.

He might break her heart when he walked away, but she would never, ever regret him.

They dipped and weaved through the asteroid field. Ahead, the moon drew nearer. More asteroids whirled past them.

Then an alarm sounded in her suit. Information flashed on her visor.

"Ashtin?"

"There is a *draarkil* incoming." He was looking around. "There!"

Kennedy turned her head, and her mouth dropped open.

Holy fucking hell.

The creature was *huge*. She watched the dragon—the *draarkil*—slowly emerge from behind a large asteroid.

It had dark scales that were almost black. It flew straight up, its wings outstretched, like a phoenix.

She was mesmerized. She'd never seen anything like it.

"Kennedy!"

Ashtin's voice snapped her back.

"We need to get to the moon. Fast. The *draarkil* will be on our tail."

The creature was already wheeling around.

"And my scans are detecting more of the creatures," he continued. "If they come at us in full force, we won't make it to the moon."

"All right. Race you to the moon, Knightmaster." Kennedy pushed more speed from her suit's propulsion system.

Ashtin moved up beside her, and they dipped past more asteroids. Alarms blared.

"Kennedy, this way." He shot straight up. She turned and followed.

And saw the terrifying sight behind them.

The black *draarkil* was hunting them. It was flying in fast, its giant wings held streamlined against its stocky, powerful body.

Her heart leaped into her throat.

She and Ashtin flew around a large asteroid, hugging the surface.

"Go, go!" he roared.

The *draarkil* was getting closer.

They needed to hit the atmosphere and get out of the path of the creature. The large *draarkil* put on a burst of speed, aiming right for her.

"Kennedy!" Ashtin yelled.

She had no time to react, but thankfully her suit whirled her around.

The *draarkil* lunged, a huge mouthful of enormous fangs snapping just a meter away from her face.

Her pulse went crazy, then her suit whirled her again and she dropped fast, barreling toward the moon's surface.

Ashtin flew up beside her and grabbed her hand.

They shot forward. She risked looking back, and saw two more *draarkil*—these ones with lighter coloring—flying out from behind an asteroid.

Her heart simply stopped. *God.*

The three *draarkil* moved into formation. They were a terrifying sight that sent a shot of adrenaline through her system.

"Ashtin, there are more of them."

"I see them." He pulled her close, their bodies locked together.

They arrowed toward Gammis III.

"Almost there," he said.

She held on to him and looked into his eyes. Some of the tension inside of her eased. They were together, whatever happened.

A second later, they hit the atmosphere.

The ride got rough.

They arrowed downward, the moon's gravity pulling on them. Her body shook, they started to spin. Dizziness swamped her and she gritted her teeth.

She couldn't lose consciousness, or she'd be dragon fodder.

Kennedy tightened her hold on Ashtin. Finally, after what felt like an eternity, she felt them slowing. Angling her head, she saw the surface of the moon was coming into clearer focus. Soon, she saw grasslands, and rocky hills in the distance.

As they barreled closer, she spotted the castle ruins.

They sat on a small, rocky rise, like an island in the sea of grassland. Most of the gray-stone structure was nothing more than tumbled rocks and ruins, but here and there, a tower or part of a structure remained standing. It made her think of the remains of an ancient, medieval castle.

"We need to deploy the wings," Ashtin said.

She nodded and released him. She fell away from his body, and a second later, her wings flared out, slowing her speed.

They flew over the grassland, and she saw some deer-like animals running below them.

Ahead, Ashtin slowed and landed, running a few steps before his suit wings retracted.

Kennedy landed nearby, not quite as gracefully as Ashtin, but she managed to stay on her feet. Her wings retracted, and her visor slid up and her helmet retracted.

She laughed. Exhilaration raced through her.

She turned to Ashtin. He was scanning the sky, then he turned to her and smiled. "No *draarkil*."

She closed the distance between them, grabbed his face, and kissed him.

"That was amazing," she said.

He ran a hand over her hair.

"Will the *draarkil* follow?" she asked, looking up into the clear, blue sky.

"They might. They prefer being in space as adults, but they are fully capable of landing on the moon."

They both turned and looked at the castle ruins.

Kennedy could easily imagine the long-ago battle that had destroyed it. Oronis knights facing off with Gek'Dragar. Blood, fighting, and chaos.

Then she gasped and grabbed his arm. "Ashtin, look." She pointed.

Up on the hill beside a ruined tower was the Uruta cruiser.

CHAPTER SEVENTEEN

The ship looked abandoned. Ashtin did a quick scan, hoping to detect two Oronis life signs.

Information filled his heads-up display, and he gritted his teeth. "The ship has a containment field protecting it. I can't scan it."

"The field must be protecting *something*," Kennedy said.

The cruiser sat in the shadow of the ruins of Castle Ishta. The highest tower still stood, mostly. The top had crumbled away long ago, but the rest still stood upright. A testament to Oronis dedication and strength.

Hope surged inside him. Carys had that same dedication and strength, as did Sten.

They were still alive. He was sure of it.

"Let's get up there," he said.

Kennedy gave a decisive nod. "Hell, yeah."

They started across the grass. He checked several times for any of the *draarkil* following, but the skies were clear.

"We'll take off the exo-suits shortly. They're made for space, and down here, they'll just slow us down."

"It weighs a ton," she agreed. "Up there, while we were flying, I felt like I didn't weigh a thing."

He heard the excitement in her voice. "We'll go for another fly once this is over and Carys is safe."

She smiled. "I'll hold you to that, Galahad."

No one had ever used a pet name for him before. It had grown on him. He liked it.

As they neared the ruins, a roar pierced the air.

They both swiveled.

The large, black *draarkil* soared through the sky, wings outspread.

Gul. The creature was majestic, but the sight of it made Ashtin's gut tighten.

"Uh-oh," Kennedy said.

Three more creatures were with it. They weren't as large, but it didn't make them any less dangerous.

"Let's move." He broke into a run.

Kennedy tried to run, but her exo-suit spine was slowing her down. He reached over and wrenched it off her. He quickly shrugged out of his, and dropped them both in the grass.

He took her hand, and they ran.

As they sprinted, the long grass slapped at their knees, tangling around their calves. The ruins of the castle were right ahead.

They were almost there.

There was another roar, and the sound of beating wings.

Kennedy looked back and her eyes went wide. "Ashtin! *Duck*."

He leaped and knocked her down, covering her body with his. The long grass enveloped them.

There was a whoosh as the *draarkil* flew past them, and he felt a wash of intense energy and a crackling noise.

Cautiously, they both lifted their heads. The grass ahead of them was burned and crackled with electricity.

"Oh, my God," she breathed.

"Up." He yanked her to her feet. The *draarkil* was wheeling through the air. "We have to get to the ruins before it returns."

Thankfully, the other three *draarkil* were staying high, soaring in circles.

Kennedy picked up speed, sprinting fast. Ashtin followed her.

Then he heard another sound. It was a throaty roar, but not as loud or deep as the *draarkil's*. It was followed by several others.

They both looked to their left. The long grass was waving madly.

Something was coming.

She sucked in a sharp breath. "What is that?"

"I don't know." He slid his black armor into place as he ran. "Keep moving."

She pumped her arms and legs.

There were so many shapes moving toward them. Whatever they were, there were a lot of them.

Ashtin and Kennedy reached the base of the ruins.

The grass ended, and they sprinted between the ruined walls and tumbled down buildings.

She gasped.

He saw her looking down. There was a skeleton, still dressed in old armor, a rusted sword resting beside it.

An Oronis knight.

In his head, Ashtin gave his thanks to the warrior of old.

As they hurried on, picking their way through the ruins of Ishta, they came across more bones, and old weapons. Several of the skeletons had large with bony tails.

A reminder of the long-ago battle with the Gek'Dragar.

Energy filled him. His ancestors had fought here. They'd given their lives to push back their enemies.

Now, it appeared that the Gek'Dragar wanted once again to attempt to destroy every last trace of the Oronis.

Ashtin wouldn't let it happen.

Not just because he was a weapon for his knightqueen and my people. Because he was Knight-master Ashtin Caydor.

He looked at the fierce woman beside him. Because he had more than just duty and honor now.

He had this woman.

A woman he loved.

Warmth rushed inside him. He'd never loved someone before. Not like this. Loving Kennedy made him stronger. It strengthened his resolve, it didn't weaken him.

He would fight. He would rescue his queen and friend. He would defend Oronis.

And he would fight for his woman.

The creatures in the grass broke free, pouring into the ruins.

His chest tightened and Kennedy just stared.

"Baby *draarkil*," she murmured.

They were younger versions of the *draarkil* in the sky. About the size of a canine, they had compact, powerful bodies, and were agile on their feet. Their wings were proportionately too small for their bodies, which probably meant they couldn't fly, yet.

"They must be breeding on the moon," he said. "The juveniles stay down here until they're old enough and strong enough to fly into space."

"So, this moon is their nest," she murmured.

More and more juvenile *draarkil* poured into the ruins like a wave.

"They still have sharp fangs and are dangerous." He knew they moved fast, and liked to hunt.

"It doesn't look like they can fly, yet. Right?"

"I don't think so. It looks like they're staying on the ground."

"Then we'll get to higher ground." She looked up. "Let's get to the tower."

Together, they swiveled and sprinted for the remains of the tower.

KENNEDY RAN FASTER than she ever had before.

Having a pack of baby dragons after you was effective motivation.

She leaped over a tumbled stone wall. In her head, she pictured this castle in its heyday. It would've been a sight to see.

"Nearly there," Ashtin said.

The tower rose ahead, the base of its staircase just visible. Despite the top being missing, the rest of it looked sturdy.

Suddenly, two young *draarkil* leaped out of the ruins, blocking their way. The creatures snarled.

Kennedy stumbled to a halt, whipping up her blaster. She was pretty sure it would be useless against these creatures. They were younger and smaller, but their hides were still scaly and tough.

One threw back its head and roared, showing off rows of shiny, spiky fangs. Long tails whipped around behind them. Both were a little different—one brown, one more red in coloring. The brown one had a large spike on the end of its tail, while the other was covered in lots of armored bumps.

Ashtin formed an energy ball and threw it. It engulfed the red *draarkil*, and it let out a deafening cry and writhed. The brown one turned, agitated, then charged them.

Kennedy leaped out of the way and fired her blaster. She aimed for the *draarkil's* face and chest. She thought the skin looked softer there.

The creature roared and raced into the ruins.

"Come on." Ashtin shoved her forward.

She looked back and saw the sea of juveniles was

getting closer.

"God, how many are there?" she panted.

"Clearly the *draarkil* have been happily breeding here."

They crossed the open space toward the base of the tower, but Kennedy realized the wave of juveniles would reach them first.

They'd be overrun.

"Ashtin—"

He stopped and whipped around. He raised his hands, both palms crackling with blue energy.

"Keep running and get to the tower, Kennedy."

Her jaw locked. *Hell, no.* She wasn't leaving him.

She leaped onto a low wall and took position.

The juveniles neared, several roaring. Most were about the size of large dogs, but some were larger.

Ashtin threw energy balls at them. Several went down under the onslaught, but more and more kept coming.

She started firing her blaster.

She heard Ashtin curse when he realized she was still there. He formed his glowing sword, then he launched himself at the closest *draarkils*.

As he whirled and slashed, blood splattered on the stones of Castle Ishta, like it had centuries ago.

Her knight sure was something to watch.

Pure death.

Kennedy growled in frustration. Her blaster wasn't doing enough damage. She spotted a sword in the rubble. It wasn't as rusted as the other ones, and the metal gleamed in the sunlight.

Like it was waiting for her.

She shoved her blaster in its holster, and picked up the sword.

She whirled, just as a *draarkil* leaped at her.

Swinging the sword up, she tightened her grip and tried to remember the lessons she'd taken. It wasn't her weapon of choice, but she'd taken several classes with Space Corps marines, who trained with combat swords.

She sliced into the *draarkil* and it screeched.

"Don't like that, do you?" She slashed again.

It ran off, limping, trailing blood behind it.

She saw another *draarkil* coming at Ashtin from behind. He was absorbed in the fight—cutting down other *draarkil*—and he hadn't noticed it.

Kennedy ran, raising her sword. She yelled, "Ashtin, watch out!"

He whirled and dodged the leaping *draarkil* at the last second.

The brown *draarkil* lunged and missed him. Kennedy rammed her sword into its hide.

It made a horrible sound, and its deep-red eyes met hers.

"Sorry, but that knight is mine. I'm not letting you hurt him."

The red glow dimmed.

Then, the creature's tail whipped around, slamming into her.

She fell, and smacked onto the hard ground. She felt something sharp pierce her suit. The dead *draarkil* rolled on top of her and she grunted.

"Kennedy!"

Then Ashtin was there. He heaved the dead creature off her.

"Are you okay?" He gripped her shoulder. "We need—"

He sucked in a breath. She looked down.

The spike on the *draarkil's* tail had pierced her side, cutting straight through her suit. Blood was pouring down her body.

Uh-oh.

He scooped her up. "You'll be fine. We'll get to the tower, and I'll stop the bleeding."

He sounded panicked. She slid her arm around his neck and held on. "Go."

Her knight ran, her weight not slowing him down. More *draarkil* gave chase, but several had stopped to eat the bodies of their downed brothers and sisters.

Kennedy winced.

They were almost at the tower.

"You'll be fine," he repeated, and she heard the hard edge in his voice.

"I will." But she was conscious of the blood pumping out of her, and she was already growing dizzy.

She didn't tell him it was getting harder to breathe. She suspected the spike had hit her lung.

She wouldn't last long.

Damn, it was so unfair. She'd finally found the one person who meant the universe to her. A man who was the ultimate adventure, but also embodied the comfort and safety of home.

A home she'd never truly had before.

She bit her lip.

Ashtin reached the base of the tower. She felt his energy gather, then he leaped straight up into the air.

He grabbed onto a tall, narrow window with one hand. Her body jerked against his and pain rocketed through her. She bit down on her tongue hard to stop from crying out.

"We're almost there, Kennedy. Hang on." He climbed into the tower.

It was a small, empty room covered in a layer of dust.

He laid her flat on the floor. He pressed a palm over her wound and applied pressure. She groaned.

"I need to stop the bleeding."

"I know," she whispered. There was so much emotion on his face. There was no sign of the cool, haughty knight she'd first met in Castle Aravena.

Then his visor slid over his face. "I'm sending out an emergency call to his people. Our ship on the asteroid will relay it across the network."

As far as she knew, there was no one close. The *Helios* was off trying to track the stealth trail with Kaden and Nea. There was no knowing exactly where they were.

Ashtin's visor retracted. He moved his hand and she saw his handsome face pale. She looked down. God, there was a lot of blood on her. She pulled in a painful breath.

"*Kennedy.*" He pressed both hands over her wound. "No. *No.*" He met her gaze, his distraught. "I can't lose you."

CHAPTER EIGHTEEN

Ashtin's heart was drumming. There was so much blood.

He brushed Kennedy's hair back from her pale face. Then he noticed the labored rasp of her breathing.

"Kennedy, I can't lose you. I won't."

"Ashtin..."

Her voice was weak. His hands tightened on her. He felt like claws were slashing at his insides. "I'm not letting you die."

"I'm not keen to die...either." She drew in a breath. "I think the spike pierced my lung." Another harsh breath.

He pressed down on her wound harder, and tried to stem the flow of blood. It coated his hands.

Pain speared through him. He could feel the life running out of her.

His Kennedy. So brave, so curious, so alive.

The thought of her dying...

He quickly unfastened her suit and pushed it open. She wore a black tank top beneath. "You got me addicted to you, Kennedy. You make me smile, you make me *feel*. I can't live without you now."

"You're an Oronis knight," she whispered. "You have your duty and honor."

He leaned over her. "Now I'm a knight in love with a brave woman from Earth."

Her eyes widened. "Ashtin." Then she groaned. "Keep...the pressure on."

He used one hand to open the pouch on his belt. He pulled out a small med kit and quickly yanked out an absorber pad. He shoved her sodden tank top up and pressed the pad over the wound. The high-tech fabric sucked up the blood and she moaned in pain.

Her breaths were becoming faster, more labored.

"Blood...trapped. Hemothorax. Ashtin, you need to... insert a chest tube, or...I'll die."

His pulse spiked.

"I took...an advanced med course."

"Of course, you did." He'd never met a more knowl-edgeable person. He pulled the soaked absorber pad off.

"Won't be able to breathe soon." She gasped. "Help...me."

His gut tightened painfully. "Whatever you need." If he had to hurt her to save her, he would.

He'd give his life for her.

He pulled out the auto-med machine. It was a small, multifunction device.

Then he heard roars echo from outside.

By the coward's bones. The *draarkil* were trying to get to them. He rose, and took a step to the window. A sea of juveniles swarmed around the tower. Several were trying to climb up the walls.

But he and Kennedy were safe for the moment. He had to help her.

He focused back on her and blocked out the sounds of the creatures. He knelt and ran the med-light over the skin of her ribs. It cleaned the blood away, showing the ragged stab wound in detail. His jaw tightened. At least the light would kill the germs and sterilize the wound.

Next, he touched the auto-med screen and printed out a small, clear tube.

He dialed up a painkiller, but stopped. "I don't know if Oronis medications will work with your physiology."

She licked her lips, her cheeks so pale. "Can't...risk it. Just make the cut."

"Kennedy—"

"I'm tough." She managed a shaky smile and moved her hand. "Cut here."

He blew out a breath, and touched the auto-med again. A thin medical blade extended.

He touched it to her skin between her ribs, but didn't cut yet. This would cause her pain.

"Do it." Her gaze locked on his. "Do it, Ashtin."

He cut into her skin.

She cried out. The sound of her pain slashed at him.

But he didn't stop. He kept cutting. More blood coated her skin.

Then it was done. Jaw so tight it hurt, he inserted the tube and pushed.

She moaned, then she slowly relaxed. Blood ran out of the tube and her harsh breathing eased.

"You...did it," she panted.

He leaned over and pressed his lips to her forehead. "Let's *never* do this again." He ran the auto-med light over her again.

But he knew she didn't have long. She was still losing blood. His temporary fix wouldn't hold her for long. She needed a knighthealer.

Suddenly, the tower shook.

His head snapped up.

"Ashtin, help me sit up. Put—" she licked her dry lips "—the blaster in my hand."

He hesitated.

Her gray eyes narrowed. "Now, Knightmaster. I'm not going to be lying on my back if some of those monsters get in here."

"You like giving orders," he grumbled.

"Only when stubborn, overprotective knights want to stop me doing what I need to do."

He helped her sit against the wall. Her bloodstained fingers clamped onto the blaster.

Ashtin strode to the window. Hundreds of *draarkil* gathered at the base of the tower, others were halfway up the wall, and several were getting very close to their window.

And that's when he saw something else that made his blood run cold.

"I just saw you tense," she said. "What is it?"

Gek'Dragar soldiers were marching into the ruins.

He closed his eyes. "The Gek'Dragar are here."

She hissed. "No."

Fueled by his terror for Kennedy—the woman who'd

captured his heart—he pulled energy to him, hard and fast. He leaned out the window, a giant ball of blue growing between his palms. He tossed his arms out.

A wave of blue energy hit the closest *draarkil* on the tower. Two creatures fell, knocking others off the walls of the tower.

Across the ruins, he watched the Gek'Dragar roaring a battle cry. As he watched, the soldiers' bodies started to change, growing larger.

The var. His jaw tightened as he saw them take warrior form, morphing into their bigger, stronger, beast-like shapes.

He heard the whine of a laser blaster behind him.

He swiveled.

A small *draarkil* had climbed in the window on the other side of the tower. Kennedy fired at it.

Gritting his teeth, he stormed across the space. He sliced an energy blade out, and it cut into the creature. It screeched.

He gripped it by the scruff of its scaled neck and tossed it out the window.

Suddenly, the tower shook wildly. Rubble from the top fell down, rushing past the windows.

Ashtin gripped the side of the window and looked up.

And saw the giant black, adult *draarkil* clamped onto the side of the tower. It let out a deafening roar.

Kennedy winced. "Daddy dropped by for a visit."

"We can't stay here." He crouched beside her, pulling her suit gently closed over her wound. "We need to jump."

She cleared her throat. "The tower is surrounded by juveniles. There are Gek'Dragar soldiers advancing. We can't fight them all. You can't fight them at all if you're holding me."

"I don't care." He slid his arms under her.

"*Ashtin.*" She cupped his cheek. "I don't want you to die. If we both go, we both die. If you go alone, you have a chance—"

"No!" Everything in him revolted at the thought. "I am *not* leaving you. We're a team. We go together."

"Ashtin," her tone was exasperated.

He pressed his palm over hers on his cheek. "I breathe for you, Kennedy. My heart beats for you. My sword, my body, my soul are now yours."

Emotion swamped her face. "Wow, I didn't know knights could be so poetic."

"You inspire it in me. I will *never* leave you."

She bit her lip. "My parents did. I never mattered enough."

"You matter to *me*. You're vital to *me*." He rose with her in his arms. "We jump, then run for the Urata ship."

"All right." She lifted her blaster. "We've got this."

"We've got this." He reached the window, gave her one last kiss, then he jumped.

KENNEDY PUSHED DOWN THE PAIN. Her side burned, and agony was crawling through her chest.

Her vision blurred, but she fought to hold on. She

wouldn't be more of a liability to Ashtin than she already was.

He landed on the dirt below, bending his knees, and the stab of pain made her bite her tongue.

He tossed off more energy balls with one hand, then headed toward the ship.

But the *draarkil* were closing in, making growling sounds and edging closer.

They didn't charge at them, though.

Kennedy frowned. *What were they waiting for?*

Then she saw.

The *draarkil* scurried back, and she watched as a line of Gek'Dragar marched forward.

They were big, muscled, and holding weapons. They looked like dragons in humanoid form with their solid, spiked tails behind them and those wicked horns on their head.

Her chest filled with a hot ball of fear. "Ashtin, the Gek'Dragar."

"I see them." He threw another blast of energy.

"Put me down. Run for the ship."

He glanced down at her. "You know I'm incapable of doing that."

"Damn you, you'll be killed!"

"I'll be with you."

His words filled her with so many clashing emotions. But deep inside, a warmth bloomed like the sun on a cloudless day.

This magnificent man loved her. Her entire life, a part of her had wondered why she was never important enough for her parents, or everyone else who'd come into her life.

But the way Ashtin held her, looked at her, and the way he risked his life for her, she knew that he would hold her close until his last breath.

A boom sounded. A Gek'Dragar weapon firing.

Ashtin dropped, curling around her. She felt a wash of energy rush over them, glowing green. Then he rose, holding her tight, and set off running.

Oh, God. It was the same weapon the Gek'Dragar had used on Oron. That affected the knights' implants.

She fired her blaster over his shoulder, but she knew it wasn't strong enough to do much damage.

Another boom, and Ashtin jolted. His hands tightened on her.

He'd been clipped. "Ashtin!" she cried.

"Not...stopping." His face twisted, but he kept moving, keeping her out of the line of fire.

Her vision wavered. *Hold on, Kennedy.* For him.

Another blast and his body shook. This time green energy skated over his skin.

His face went blank, but she saw the pain boiling in his eyes. He stayed upright, but swayed.

"I love you." Tears fell down her cheeks.

He was walking unsteadily now, but he took another step, and another.

But the Gek'Dragar fired again, and he stumbled.

Her brave knight.

Refusing to let her go, refusing to go down.

The Gek'Dragar moved closer, starting to circle around them.

"Tell me you love me, my knightmaster."

"With every breath. With every swing of my sword." His blue eyes glittered. "With every beat of my heart."

In her periphery, the Gek'Dragar were lifting their weapons. She gripped Ashtin tighter.

There was a blast of blue light.

She squeezed her eyes shut, waiting for the pain.

There was another blast of blue.

Nothing happened. She opened her eyes. An Oronis knight was standing between them and the Gek'Dragar.

The knight was in full armor, and had formed two glowing, blue swords. The knight attacked.

It was Nea.

More Oronis knights winked into existence, teleporting across the battlefield.

Hope punched through Kennedy.

The Oronis knights were here.

Even more appeared, charging in to attack the Gek'Dragar.

Another knight appeared in a ball of red light, right beside them. She frowned. *Red light?*

It was Kaden.

"Easy." The knighthunter caught Ashtin before he fell. "It's going to be okay. Hand her to me."

"No." Ashtin's arms tightened on her. "She needs a knighthealer."

"So do you. Your back is torn to shreds."

Kennedy made a sound, fighting to stay conscious. "Ashtin..."

"No," he clipped.

Kaden's lips quirked. "He's had worse, don't worry."

A Gek'Dragar soldier broke free of the line and ran at them.

Without a sound, Kaden whirled and stomped a foot down. He threw one arm forward.

Three giant spikes of red energy flew from him toward the Gek'Dragar.

Kennedy blinked. Unlike the other knights, Kaden's energy was a deep red.

The spikes grew in size, then impaled the Gek'Dragar.

"For the knightqueen!" someone yelled.

"For the knightqueen! For the Oronis!" The knights around the battlefield echoed the cry.

Knights charged and whirled, a deadly force. She watched them, and spotted Nea standing on a wall. The female knight no longer held swords. Instead, she held a deadly-looking bow and was firing bolts of blue energy at the enemy.

It didn't take long before the Gek'Dragar were in retreat. Even the *draarkil* were flying away, while the juveniles fled on foot.

There was a boom in the sky.

A huge, black ship appeared, firing on the adult *draarkil*.

Ashtin sat down heavily, holding Kennedy in his lap. "Knighthealer. *Now.*"

A moment later, there was a blink of blue light, and a woman in armor appeared.

"Knightmaster Ashtin." The woman hurried over to them.

"Knighthealer Taera." There was relief on his handsome face. "Heal her. *Now*."

"Check him over," Kennedy rasped. "I know his back is hurt, but he won't let me see."

"She's lost a lot of blood. And her lung was damaged."

The healer shook her head. "Quiet, both of you. I'll heal you both. Now, sit still."

They both nodded.

"You didn't let go," Kennedy whispered.

Ashtin pressed his face to her hair. "I never will."

"But you need to go and search that Urata ship. You need to find Knightqueen Carys."

His arms tightened. "Someone else will do it. I'm right where I need to be."

Kennedy closed her eyes and pressed her face against his neck as the knighthealer started her work.

CHAPTER NINETEEN

He held Kennedy as the knighthealer worked on her. In fact, Ashtin might never let her go.

He felt her body tense, her muscles shaking. He knew that healing could hurt. He'd been patched up by the knighthealers too many times to count.

Knighthealer Taera from the *BlackBlade* was one of the best. Her implants were geared toward directing energy to heal.

Most importantly, Ashtin knew that Kennedy was going to be okay.

He pulled her closer, ignoring his own pain.

Kennedy lifted her gaze and her expression softened. A second later, her eyes glazed over. "Oh, that doesn't hurt anymore. It feels *good*."

Knighthealer Taera smiled. Healing affected everyone differently.

"I feel warm and fluffy now," Kennedy said with a slow smile.

"She's all healed," Taera said, closing up Kennedy's suit. "She needs fluids, nutrients, and rest."

"I'll make sure she gets them."

"Because you take care of me," Kennedy said. "Whether I want it or not."

"That's right." He stroked her cheekbone.

Taera moved to his back and let out a low hiss.

He could feel how bad his injuries were from the Gek'Dragar weapon. His combat implants had blocked most of the pain, but it was still agony.

Even now, he wasn't sure how he'd stayed conscious.

The healer started work, and Ashtin kept his focus on Kennedy.

"Thanks for saving me," she murmured.

"I will always save you."

"I know."

He leaned down and kissed her. He felt Taera jerk in surprise. His knights had never seen him with a woman. Kennedy made a hum of pleasure. When he looked up, Taera was smiling at him.

"You're all healed, Ashtin."

"Thanks, Taera."

"Ashtin," Kennedy said. "I love you."

He'd heard her, in the midst of trying to escape the Gek'Dragar, but a part of him hadn't quite believed it. "No one ever has before."

She cupped his cheek. "I'll love you so hard, you'll never, ever remember what it feels like not to be loved."

"And I love you, Kennedy. You'll never, ever remember what it feels like to be left behind."

"Are you two all right?" Nea strode over, her dark

armor splattered with gore.

He had to force himself to drag his attention off Kennedy.

"We're fine now," he replied, helping Kennedy stand. She was a little unsteady, but there was color in her cheeks now.

"We got your emergency call," Nea said.

"I wasn't sure it would reach you," he said.

"It wouldn't have, except someone boosted the signal from your ship." Nea frowned. "There were a few frantic beeping noises added to the message."

Kennedy laughed. "Oh my God. *Beep*. He must have boosted the signal."

Ashtin would give the drone whatever he wanted. "I'm glad you made it in time, Nea."

"We shouldn't have. We were in the Naxos quadrant, still trying to follow that damn trail."

He frowned. The Naxos quadrant was a long way from Gammis III. Too far. "How did you make it here in time?"

"It seems our knighthunter was hiding some secrets." Nea's voice was sharp as she flicked a glance over her shoulder.

Kaden appeared, sauntering toward them. The sunlight turned his platinum-hair silver. His gaze raked over Kennedy and Ashtin before he looked at Nea. "That's the job of a knighthunter. To keep secrets."

"Secrets from your *enemy*," Nea said. "Not your own people."

Kaden shrugged.

"We made it in time to save you two because

Knighthunter Galath teleported the *BlackBlade* here," Nea said.

Ashtin raised a brow. He knew Kaden had unique abilities that most knights didn't have. He also knew that Kaden could teleport, but not entire ships.

"He did the same with the Earth ship," Nea added. "It's here as well, in orbit. They're keeping the *draarkil* clear of Gammis III. "He then teleported all our knights down to the surface." She sounded like she couldn't quite believe it.

Kaden smiled. "If you want all my secrets, Knight-master Laurier, you just have to ask nicely."

Nea sniffed, then turned to face the Uruta cruiser.

"That's the ship that left Kravaa III with the knightqueen aboard," Ashtin told them.

Kaden crossed his arms over his chest. "It has a containment field around it."

Ashtin nodded. "We need to take the field down and get on that ship."

"We need that containment field deactivated." Nea waved a hand, and two knights approached the ship. She barked orders at them, and a moment later, one of them pulled out a device. They stuck a metal spike into the field, energy sparking. Then the other tapped on a screen.

A second later, there was a bright shimmer, and the containment barrier flicked off.

"Scanning now," Nea said.

But Ashtin already knew that there would be no life signs aboard.

He took Kennedy's hand, and they approached the ship. Nea and Kaden flanked them.

The door of the ship opened, and a ramp lowered. They walked up.

Inside, it looked like a standard Uruta cruiser decorated in a deep red. The Uruta liked their luxuries. The seats were big and plush, and polished metal lined the cabinetry. The cockpit and seating areas were all empty.

The back of the ship had been retrofitted with cells.

His jaw tightened.

The cells were empty; the door of one standing open. He stepped inside, and Kennedy circled the space.

"There's nothing here," she said. "Dammit, we don't even know if they were on this ship."

"We'll search the ship's computer system," Nea said. "And there might be a security feed. Something that will give us a clue."

Ashtin knew everything would've been erased.

Disappointment hit. It mingled with worry for his queen and friend. He had no idea where to look for them next.

"Wait, what's this?" Kennedy crouched by a bench attached to the wall.

He stepped forward, and saw her touch a mark engraved in the wall. He crouched and sucked in a breath.

Kennedy frowned. "It's a straight line with two triangles over it. Like mountains."

"No, it's a crown. A sword and crown. The symbol for the knightqueen. They were here. And they were alive."

"They must have been moved from the moon to somewhere else," Kaden said.

"They could still be on Gammis III," Kennedy said.

"We've already scanned the moon," Nea said. "The only Oronis life sign before we arrived was Ashtin. But we'll check again. The *BlackBlade* is currently scanning for any remaining Gek'Dragar. Their ship has already been destroyed."

Ashtin frowned, wondering where Carys and Sten could have gone.

Kennedy touched his hand, and he caught her fingers and squeezed.

"We won't give up," she said.

He nodded.

"Wait." Kaden touched the side of his visor. "I have a comm call incoming from Captain Attaway on the *Helios*." He paused. "Go ahead, Captain. I'm with Knightmasters Nea and Ashtin, and Sub-Captain Black."

"I hope everyone is all right," the captain's voice came through clearly. "Kaden, we've picked up a new stealth trail. It's made from the same generator of the trail we were tracking previously from Oron."

Ashtin straightened. "A Gek'Dragar ship. And the trail leaves Gammis III?"

"Yes. My engineers are working to increase the tracking capabilities, but I'm one hundred percent certain another ship recently left the moon."

Kennedy smiled. "We just got a trail to follow."

IT WAS nice to be back on the *Helios*.

Eve, who'd been standing with Davion, Douglas,

Claudine, and the captain, strode across the bridge and hugged Kennedy. Captain Attaway nodded at her.

"Well done, Kennedy," the captain said. "Thanks to you, you single-handedly proved Earth's innocence, and cemented our alliance with the Oronis."

"I just did what was right. We still need to find Knightqueen Carys."

"We'll all work together to do that," Davion said from Eve's side. "We're not letting the Gek'Dragar get away with this. And Carys is strong and smart. Plus, her best guard is with her."

If they were still alive.

Ashtin appeared at Kennedy's side. "Feeling all right?" He stroked her back.

She smiled up at him. "I'm fine. Quit hovering."

God, this man was *hers*. He loved her. She saw it right now, shining in his eyes.

He gave her hair a stroke, then turned to Captain Attaway.

"Captain, can you show us what you have on the ship that left the moon?"

"Of course, Knightmaster."

They all turned to face the light table set on one side of the bridge. Nea and Kaden joined them.

"Well, well." Claudine leaned close to Kennedy with a smile. "Someone followed my advice and jumped on that magnificent man."

Kennedy felt heat in her cheeks, but she smiled.

On the other side of Claudine, Eve grinned. "You fell for the knightmaster, huh? And by the way he looks at you, he's not letting you go."

Kennedy felt a niggle in her belly. "I have no idea how we'll make this work." She felt a rush of nerves. Maybe a part of her expected him to change his mind. "I'm a Space Corps xenoanthropologist, and he's an Oronis knight..."

Eve grabbed her hand and smiled. "Take it from someone who's been in your situation. You'll find a way to make it work. Love finds a way."

Kennedy watched as the woman glanced at Davion, her face filled with love.

They gathered at the light table. Kennedy moved to Ashtin's side, and he instantly wrapped an arm around her.

She saw Kaden's lips twitch, while Nea frowned at them.

"Here's what we detected," Captain Attaway said.

On-screen was the trail of a ship leaving Gammis III.

It was faint, but it was there.

"We estimate it was about six hours before Knight-master Ashtin and Sub-Captain Black arrived," the *Helios'* nav officer said.

"Damn," Kennedy muttered. They'd been so close.

"We will *not* give up on our knightqueen," Ashtin said. "Or Knightguard Sten. They are Oronis knights, and they will fight to survive."

"And we *will* get them back," Nea said, resolve in her voice.

"Chief Engineer Watson, how is your work progressing on strengthening your ability to track the stealth trail?" Ashtin asked.

"It's coming along." The older woman shrugged. "I

wish I could tell you that we've nailed it, ah, that's an Earth term. We haven't found a way to successfully boost the tracking, yet. Every step forward, we hit a snag." The engineer glanced at Kaden. "Knightmaster Kaden is helping my team. He's surprisingly not bad."

Kaden smiled. "Your gushing praise is almost embarrassing, Chief."

The woman snorted. There was a clear camaraderie between the two. "Something tells me that you don't need more praise."

"That actually is high praise from the chief," Kennedy said.

"The knighthunter has given us a few ideas, and some Oronis tech that we're integrating into our system." The chief stabbed a finger at the map on the light table. "I'm certain we'll come up with a way to track these asshole Gek'Dragar down."

"Then let's get to work," Kaden said.

"We *must* find that ship," Ashtin said.

"We will find the knightqueen," Nea said. "Whatever it takes."

"Let's all get to work." Captain Attaway glanced at Ashtin and Kennedy. "Your knighthealer has sent word. You two are to eat and rest."

Ashtin didn't look happy about the directive.

"You are no good to us if you're tired and weak," Nea said.

"Nea, can you please retrieve our ship from the asteroid field?" he asked.

"Beep will be going crazy by now," Kennedy said.

"I've already sent a team," the female knight replied.

"Come on." Kennedy took his hand. "Let's get a snack from the kitchens, and I'll give you a tour of the ship."

He looked like he wanted to argue, but he left the bridge with her.

They stopped and grabbed some food from the kitchen, and she took him to the observation deck.

It gave them a perfect view of Ashtin's ship. The *BlackBlade* was the perfect name for it.

It was pure black, and covered in spikes. The forked bow of the ship had a blue ball of energy crackling in the center of it.

"It's a hell of a ship, Ashtin." One day, Space Corps might have similar designs. As they continued to explore, and learn, and make alliances, they would grow and expand.

"After this is all over—" he ate a mouthful of some of the beef stir fry she'd nabbed for them "—after Carys and Sten are home, I'll give you a tour of my ship." He met her gaze. "And maybe you'll think about staying on it, and coming with me."

Her heart jolted. "On missions?"

"I want you with me, Kennedy." He grabbed her hand. "I don't think I can live without you."

She set her fork down. "I want to be with you, too, Ashtin."

"That's all I want."

She crawled onto his lap, and then they were kissing.

Right there in his arms, with his mouth on hers, everything felt right.

"I love you, Kennedy Black. We'll work out the logistics of being together." He nibbled on her bottom lip. "We belong together."

"*Yes.*"

"Stay with me? Let me show you Oronis space, and more."

"What I need most is you. And yes, I'll stay."

He rose with her in his arms, abandoning their food. "Now, I want to see your cabin."

Thankfully, it wasn't far, since she couldn't take her hands or mouth off her delicious knightmaster.

They stumbled down the corridor, and finally into her cabin.

"Do you want the tour?" she panted.

"Later."

He lay her on the bed, tearing at her clothes, then his.

When his bare skin touched hers, she moaned. His hands moved down her side, right where she'd been injured.

"I'm all right," she told him.

"I know." He pressed a kiss to her ribs, then he nudged her thighs apart. His big body covered hers and he surged inside her.

Kennedy arched up, crying out his name. "*Yes.* God, I keep thinking this is all a dream."

"It's not a dream. I'm yours, Kennedy."

"Love me, Ashtin."

"*Always.* This is where I belong."

Then he started thrusting faster, and Kennedy held onto the man she loved, and lost herself in the pleasure.

CHAPTER TWENTY

Ashtin was feeling very good.

He was in love.

He could never have understood how all-consuming it would feel. Or how it would motivate him to be more, to do more, to be better.

And yet, he knew Kennedy loved him. Just as he was. She didn't need him to be anything other than himself. She respected the knightmaster, but she loved the man.

He wanted to give her everything—to ensure her safety, give her interesting experiences, to give her pleasure and happiness.

"Look at you. Smiling and happy." Kaden appeared out of nowhere.

"It feels good," Ashtin told his friend.

"I wouldn't know."

"You could try it."

Kaden grunted.

"Being in love... It's nothing like I imagined. It's *everything*."

"I'm not built for love, Ashtin. To borrow a word I've learned from these Terrans, I'm an asshole."

Ashtin shook his head at his friend. "That's because that's what you want people to believe. There's more to you, and we both know it. You're loyal, and you care."

Kaden made a scoffing noise. "You're kidding yourself."

"I know the boy who saved me from the River Camlann when we were nine years old cared."

"I was tempted to let you drown."

"But you didn't. And you are capable of love, if you try it."

Kaden fell silent.

Ashtin watched his friend carefully. "It might take a fight to bring her around, but it'd be worth it. I promise you."

His friend stared right at him, ice-blue eyes unblinking. "I've no idea what you're talking about."

"You're usually a better liar than that."

Fast footsteps echoed down the corridor. Kennedy appeared. Beep was hovering over her left shoulder. The drone had been sticking close to her since he'd come aboard.

"Hey, the chief has an update. Bridge. Now. Both of you." She swiveled.

They followed her to the bridge.

Chief Engineer Watson stood by the light table, her dark-gray hair pulled up in an untidy bun. She was grinning at the captain. When she saw them, her smile got impossibly wider. "We bloody did it!"

"What?" Ashtin asked.

"We added some Oronis tech to our system, and we *finally* worked it out. We can track the stealth trail of the Gek'Dragar ship." She swiped the light table.

The image showed the trail of a ship, bright and strong.

"You can track it the entire way?" Kaden asked.

"All the way, Knighthunter, if we get close enough."

"We can find our queen," Nea breathed.

"Let's see the trail," Ashtin said.

"It's blindingly bright and obvious, but we lose it here when it goes out of range." The captain swiped the screen. "But if we follow, we can keep tracking it."

Ashtin stared at the bright trail. The star map zoomed out.

Then he, Kaden, and Nea all cursed at once.

Kennedy pressed a hand to the table. "Damn, the trail crosses over into Gek'Dragar space."

"Yes," Ashtin said.

"And if an Oronis ship flies across the border, the Gek'Dragar fleet would descend with a vengeance," Nea said. "They have tech designed to detect our ships."

Ashtin stared at the floor, thinking of Carys and Sten.

"What about a ship from Earth?" Kennedy said. "One running on stealth mode that the Gek'Dragar can't detect?"

He looked up, saw Kennedy trade a glance with Captain Attaway. The captain nodded.

Douglas stepped forward. "Our alliance is new, but whatever Earth can do to assist the Oronis, we will. The Gek'Dragar targeted us. Now, they are our enemy, too."

"It'll be dangerous," Ashtin warned. "This trail will

go deep into Gek'Dragar territory. If the ship is caught, or something goes wrong..."

Silence fell, and everyone looked pensive.

There was a chance they wouldn't come home.

"It's the right thing to do," Kennedy said. "We have to bring the knightqueen and her guard home, no matter what."

Ashtin felt a surge of adrenaline. "We just send a skeleton crew to run the ship, and a small Oronis contingent. Captain, your people need to volunteer. They need to understand the gravity of this mission. They might not return."

Captain Attaway nodded. "My crew is the best. We'll have the key members we need."

He nodded. "And I'll put together a team—"

"Ashtin," Nea said. "There's unrest building back on Oron. Word has spread that the knightqueen has been taken by the Gek'Dragar. Plus, there are still Gek'Dragar incursions along the border."

He frowned at her. "The sooner we can rescue Carys, the better."

"You've done your bit. You and Kennedy. The people of Oron need the head of the Knightforce there to reassure them and keep the peace."

"They need you, Ashtin," Kaden said. "Besides, this kind of mission is more in my skill set."

Nea whipped around. "No, I should go. It will need a cool head and my knowledge of the Gek'Dragar."

Kaden snorted. "You just want to be in charge and steal the action."

Ashtin listened to the pair bicker. He wanted to go. He wanted to be doing something to save his queen.

Kennedy took his hand. There was understanding and support in her eyes. Whatever he chose, she'd be right beside him.

"You'll both go," Ashtin said.

Kaden and Nea glared at him. Both opened their mouths.

He held up a hand. "As you've just reminded me, I'm head of the Knightforce. Without the queen, I am in charge. Captain Attaway, once a skeleton crew is assembled, Knighthunter Kaden and Knightmaster Nea will go with you on the mission."

Ashtin looked at Kennedy. "I'll return to Oron to reassure my people, and ensure that the Gek'Dragar don't get any ideas about attacking because they think we're vulnerable."

"King Gayel has already ordered the *Desteron* to Oron to help," Davion said.

The flagship of the Eon fleet would be a huge help. "Thanks, Davion."

"And I'm coming with you, Ashtin." Kennedy said. "We're a team, remember?"

Captain Attaway nodded. "I'll need someone to return with my crewmembers who won't go on the mission. Ensure they get back to Earth."

"Consider it done," Kennedy said.

"SUB-CAPTAIN BLACK, I'm happy to see you all in one piece."

Kennedy sat in front of the comp screen in an office just off the bridge of the *Helios*, looking at her boss, Admiral William Zhang.

Ashtin was helping Kaden and Nea prepare for the mission. The crew of the *Helios* who were not going on the mission to Gek'Dragar space were being transferred to the *BlackBlade* to rendezvous with the *Desteron* at Oron.

A few key members, including Captain Attaway and Chief Engineer Watson, would stay aboard the *Helios*.

"I'm happy to be in one piece, sir," Kennedy said.

"I hear you single-handedly saved the reputation of Earth, aided the Oronis, and forged a solid alliance."

"I just wanted to prove we weren't involved with the Gek'Dragar."

"Well done. You are a credit to Space Corps, Kennedy. One of the best I've ever had in my command."

"Thank you, sir. It means a lot." She took a deep breath, fighting her conflicting emotions. "But, I need to submit my resignation."

Admiral Zhang's dark eyebrows drew together. "Resignation?"

"Well, over the course of my mission with Knight-master Ashtin...we've become close."

Now her boss' dark eyebrows went up. "I've seen the knightmaster on a comms call. A cool man. A dangerous man."

Kennedy smiled. "He can be those things, but not

with me. We're in a relationship, and it's serious. I've never felt this way about someone before."

The admiral shook his head. "What is it with these alien men snapping up our women?"

"I took a look at plenty of men on Earth, sir. Apparently, I needed to leave our solar system and find myself an alien knight. I'm in love with him."

"I'm happy for you, Kennedy. Now, there's no way I want to lose one of our best. Our alliance is new, and we could do with a Space Corps liaison to the Oronis."

Kennedy straightened. "Really?"

"Yes. We want to share information. I need you to document what you learn, send information back and forth."

"Sir, I... That would be perfect."

"Excellent. We'll do some work to put together exactly what the role will look like. Until then, support the Oronis to find the knightqueen. And if Ambassador James needs help, I expect you to be there for him."

"Of course. Thank you, Admiral."

Her boss smiled. "And make sure that knight of yours keeps you happy."

"Oh, he does. Goodbye."

The screen went black, and Kennedy jumped up with an excited squeal.

She got to stay with Space Corps, and do a job she loved, and live on Oron with Ashtin.

It was a dream come true.

The door opened.

"Are you all right?" Ashtin frowned at her.

"I am *awesome*." She held her arms out. "You're

looking at the new Space Corps liaison to the Oronis. Stationed on Oron... With the knightmaster's permission, of course."

He gave her a wide, sexy smile.

She skirted the desk and jumped on him. She kissed him wildly, and it was filled with all the emotions bubbling inside her.

"God, you're handsome," she murmured.

"I'm glad you think so."

"Fancy another quick look at my cabin?" She raked her teeth down his neck. "You never did get that tour."

"And I doubt I would now, either." He groaned and squeezed her ass. "We're due to transfer to the *Black-Blade*. I need to say goodbye to Kaden and Nea, and Captain Attaway."

"Okay." Kennedy slid her feet back to the floor, trying to get herself under control. Then she smiled at him. "Once we're on the *BlackBlade*, maybe you can give me a tour of *your* cabin?" She ran her fingers down his chest.

He grabbed her hand. "If I can wait that long. You're always too much of a temptation."

She loved knowing she tempted her knight like no one else.

"And Kennedy, it will be *our* cabin."

CHAPTER TWENTY-ONE

Nea walked into the gym on the *Helios*, needing to burn off some energy.

The start of a mission always left her revved, her mind whirring with information, plans, and worries. She liked to have some back-up plans in place, to anticipate anything that could go wrong.

This mission was so important, but added to that was the fact that they were headed into a dangerous unknown. Gek'Dragar territory. There wasn't much she could plan.

But she could be focused and ready.

She looked around. This gym wasn't what she was used to, but it would do.

She moved into a stretch. She needed to be ready for anything.

They *would* find Knightqueen Carys. Nea needed to be prepared to rescue her and bring her home.

Taking a breath, Nea moved into a series of kicks, her

body warming. At first, she moved slowly, not utilizing her combat implants.

She dropped, swiped out her leg, then leaped up. Then she activated her implants.

She moved faster, a lethal blur. She kicked, hit, and spun.

After a roll, she came to her feet in a fighting stance, breathing fast.

"You always were impressive to watch in training."

She controlled her jolt, her jaw tightening.

The man always appeared like a wraith. He'd done it at the Academy, as well. Kaden always loved making an appearance.

She moved over to the refresh station and poured herself a drink of water.

"Going to ignore me?" She heard him cross the mats. "You can't ignore me for the entire mission."

"I can try." She drank, taking her time. Then she set the cup down and turned.

He was always a hit to the system. She hated that her body noticed how he looked and reacted to it.

She let herself take in the near-white hair, the sharp cheekbones, the strong jaw, and the full lips. Lips far too sensuous for such a harsh face.

And those ice-blue eyes.

He'd been a bully at the Academy. He'd taunted her for being too studious, too serious, and always following the rules.

Kaden had always broken the rules and gotten away with it. She'd hated it.

He annoyed her on the deepest level.

"Come on now, Nea," he said. "We're adults, Oronis knights on an important mission."

"Saving Knightqueen Carys is all that matters. I'll work with you, I'll do my job. That doesn't mean I have to like it."

He stalked closer, and she fought not to tense, or take a step back.

Don't let him get to you.

He circled her, his voice a low drawl. "Maybe you will like it, Nea."

His deep voice shivered through her, and she lifted her chin. "You break the rules when it suits you, you disappear in a blink, you lie, you omit the truth. I don't trust you, Kaden."

"I've grown up. I'm not the boy who used to pull your braids at the Academy anymore."

"Who tormented and teased me, you mean. I don't think you grew up. You still do whatever you want."

He stepped even closer, their bodies barely a whisper apart.

She smelled him—a dark and spicy scent. Her belly clenched.

Ignore him. Ignore him.

"I do my duty," he said. "I do it my way. I fight in the dark and the dirt so people like you don't have to."

She frowned. "People like me?"

His eyes darkened, leaking a lethal intensity. "People who follow the rules. Who are all light and goodness." He stared at her for a beat, then stepped back. The intensity bled away from his eyes, and he grinned. "You wouldn't last one day in my world."

She snorted. "And you wouldn't last one day in mine."

"Regardless, we have to work together to find Knightqueen Carys, and bring her and Sten home. And while we do that, I'll keep you safe."

Her pulse skittered and she frowned. "I don't need you to keep me safe, Galath. I do that for myself."

He just smiled. An infuriating curl of those sensual lips.

She shoved him. "I mean it. Don't get in my way."

He grabbed her wrist and yanked her close. "Maybe I want to get in your way."

"I detest you, remember?"

He made an unconvinced sound, and it triggered her temper. Nea broke his hold on her wrist and attacked.

Of course, he was a well-trained, sneaky knighthunter, so he dodged. The man was a talented fighter.

They traded blows, moving across the mat. She kicked at him, and in a blinding-fast move, he caught her leg and yanked.

She went down. She'd half rolled when his body hit hers, pinning her to the mat on her back.

"You always fight dirty," she snapped.

His face was close to hers, his big, lean body pressed against her.

"I always fight to win. No matter what." His gaze traced her face.

Nea rolled and executed a quick flip. She pinned him down and straddled his hips. "We will do our duty and find the knightqueen, but other than that, stay out of my way." She glared at him, then rose.

Kaden smiled at her, staying sprawled on the mat like he was taking a nap. He tucked his hands under his head. "No promises, Laurier. I never make them."

"Because you never keep them." She headed for the door.

She needed some space between her and this man.

"Maybe because I've never wanted to make them. Before now."

She had no idea what he meant, but she refused to look back.

Nea strode out of the gym, determined not to let the annoying knighthunter under her skin.

"SEND an extra ship to the border at Gashminning." Ashtin looked up. He was sitting at the head of a meeting table in Castle Aravena.

A team of knights looked back at him.

"Yes, Knightmaster," one of them replied, tapping on a comp screen.

"How is the training of the new batch of guards progressing?" Ashtin asked.

A woman leaned forward. "They're coming along well. The new recruits look good."

"Excellent. Any word from the *BlackBlade*?"

His ship was currently under the command of his second, Knightmaster Tenin, and sticking close to the

Gek'Dragar border, in case Nea and Kaden sent any communications from the *Helios*.

Another knight shook her head. "No word yet."

A somber mood fell around the table. They were all thinking of their queen.

Ashtin had been back on Oron for two days. He knew it was too soon for news, but he kept hoping.

It felt strange to be so happy and so worried at the same time.

"How is general morale in the city?"

"People are concerned for the knightqueen," a man said. "We all are."

"But things have improved since you've returned." A female knight grinned. "People are *very* curious about Sub-Captain Black. The Terran woman who captured the knightmaster."

He frowned. He hated being the subject of gossip, but still, if it helped people keep their minds from their missing queen...

He rose. "Very well. Good work. Dismissed."

He decided it was time to find his woman.

Ashtin checked the nearby office he'd assigned to her, but found it empty. It already felt like Kennedy, though. There were photos on the wall, a stack of old books on the desk, and an open tablet on standby. She'd no doubt been poring over Oronis records and taking notes. He breathed in. It smelled like her. Honeysuckle. His new favorite scent.

He saw a framed picture of the two of them on her desk. Beep had taken it just after they'd returned to the castle. Ashtin was smiling, and she was laughing.

In the darkest of times, he'd found the light of his life.

He considered checking their apartment in the castle, but she was rarely there in the daytime.

At night however, they were making it their home. Last night, she'd taught him to cook an Earth meal called spaghetti carbonara. She made him laugh. And in their bed at night, he lost himself in her.

Every time he touched her, he discovered something new. Ashtin knew he'd never get tired of hearing her cry out his name as she came. Never get tired of her telling him that she loved him.

He strode onto the balcony, suspecting he knew where she'd be.

He scanned the grounds, and spotted her in the castle gardens below, a camera in her hand. Beep whizzed around her.

He could take the stairs down, but it would take too long. He gripped the railing and leaped over the balcony.

As he landed near her, she had the camera aimed his way. Beep whirled around him happily and butted against his arm. Ashtin gave the drone a pat.

She smiled. "My man is a bit of a showoff."

"Just for you." He kissed her lips.

"Any news from the *Helios*?" she asked.

"Nothing yet." He hugged her. "We aren't giving up hope. They'll find Carys and Sten. They'll bring them home."

"I know. I need some patience, but as you know, I don't have a lot of it." She cocked her head. "So Knight-master, are you on your lunch break?"

He pulled her closer. "I am. Did you have something in mind?"

"I was thinking we could go into the city. You could show me the Oronis Heritage Museum that I've heard so much about. It's filled with Oronis history, including some artifacts from Gammis III."

He smoothed her hair back. "Anything my woman wants."

She pressed closer. "We could take a transport, maybe make out a little on the way there?"

Desire throbbed. "I am at your service until I stop breathing. It would be my honor to be yours and love you for eternity."

"God, I love it when you use the fancy, poetic words. I love you, Ashtin." She pressed her lips to his.

He kissed her back, tuning out Beep's excited chirps, and then there was nothing but Kennedy, his soulmate from Earth.

Ahead of them, they had their future—one of adventure, laughter, and love. One they'd make together.

CARYS TRIED to open her eyes.

Pain.

A clanging noise.

A deep groan.

She swam through the agony and dizziness, managing to squeeze her eyes open.

Everything was a blur.

Dark rock.

Dripping water.

Pain all through her entire body.

She saw that she was dressed in a tattered, gold gown. Her bare feet were stained with dirt. There was blood on her arm.

What had happened?

One word shot into her head.

Gek'Dragar.

Horrible images slammed into her. Her chest locked and she moaned.

They'd attacked the castle.

They'd taken her.

They'd beaten her.

She had no idea where she was, or how long she'd been there. She couldn't even remember how she'd gotten here.

There was something tight on her wrist.

She tugged at it, but she could barely move. She managed to tilt her head, setting off a splitting headache.

A glowing line wrapped around her wrist. She followed it and realized it attached her to a thicker wrist, and a large, masculine hand.

She sucked in a breath. She *knew* those strong, scarred fingers.

She'd stared at them a lot. Dreamed about them touching her.

She slowly shifted her gaze. Sten was lying on the stone floor beside her. His shirt was ripped, his face beaten and covered in bruises.

No. "*Sten.*" The word was barely a whisper.

Darkness was tugging at her again.

Was he alive? The pain that cut through her at the thought that he was dead was worse than that from her injuries.

He'd always been there for her. Protecting her. Shielding her. Comforting her. He couldn't be dead.

Then Carys saw his chest move. *He was alive.*

Relief filled her.

She had no idea where they were, but she wasn't alone. Sten was with her.

She blinked, the pain eating at her.

Then, a dark whirlpool pulled and pulled at her, dragging her back under. Into nothingness.

I hope you enjoyed Kennedy and Ashtin's story!

Oronis Knights continues with *Knighthunter*, starring Knighthunter Kaden and Knightmaster Nea. Coming July 2023.

Want to find out about Sub-Captain Eve Traynor abducting War Commander Davion Thann-Eon? Check out the first book in the **Eon Warriors**, *Edge of Eon*.
Read on for a preview of the first chapter.

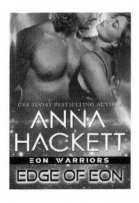

PREVIEW: EDGE OF EON

S he shifted on the chair, causing the chains binding her hands to clank together. Eve Traynor snorted. The wrist and ankle restraints were overkill. She was on a low-orbit prison circling Earth. Where the fuck did they think she was going to go?

Eve shifted her shoulders to try to ease the tension from having her hands tied behind her back. For the millionth time, she studied her surroundings. The medium-sized room was empty, except for her chair. Everything from the floor to the ceiling was dull-gray metal. All of the Citadel Prison was drab and sparse. She'd learned every boring inch of it the last few months.

One wide window provided the only break in the otherwise uniform space. Outside, she caught a tantalizing glimpse of the blue-green orb of Earth below.

Her gut clenched and she drank in the sight of her home. Five months she'd been locked away in this prison. Five months since her life had imploded.

She automatically thought of her sisters. She sucked in a deep breath. She hated everything they'd had to go through because of what had happened. Hell, she thought of her mom as well, even though their last contact had been the day after Eve had been imprisoned. Her mom had left Eve a drunken, scathing message.

The door to the room opened, and Eve lifted her chin and braced.

When she saw the dark-blue Space Corps uniform, she stiffened. When she saw the row of stars on the lapel, she gritted her teeth.

Admiral Linda Barber stepped into the room, accompanied by a female prison guard. The admiral's hair was its usual sleek bob of highlighted, ash-blonde hair. Her brown eyes were steady.

Eve looked at the guard. "Take me back to my cell."

The admiral lifted a hand. "Please leave us."

The guard hesitated. "That's against protocol, ma'am—"

"It'll be fine." The admiral's stern voice said she was giving an order, not making a request.

The guard hesitated again, then ducked through the door. It clicked closed behind her.

Eve sniffed. "Say what you have to say and leave."

Admiral Barber sighed, taking a few steps closer. "I know you're angry. You have a right to be—"

"You think?" Eve sucked back the rush of molten anger. "I got tossed under the fucking starship to save a mama's boy. A mama's boy who had no right to be in command of one of Space Corps' vessels."

Shit. Eve wanted to pummel something. Preferably the face of Robert J. Hathaway—golden son of Rear-Admiral Elisabeth Hathaway. A man who, because of family connections, was given captaincy of the *Orion*, even though he lacked the intelligence and experience needed to lead it.

Meanwhile, Eve—a Space Corps veteran—had worked her ass off during her career in the Corps, and had been promised her own ship, only to be denied her chance. Instead, she'd been assigned as Hathaway's second-in-command. To be a glorified babysitter, and to actually run the ship, just without the title and the pay raise.

She'd swallowed it. Swallowed Hathaway's incompetence and blowhard bullshit. Until he'd fucked up. Big-time.

"The Haumea Incident was regrettable," Barber said.

Eve snorted. "Mostly for the people who died. And definitely for me, since I'm the one shackled to a chair in the Citadel. Meanwhile, I assume Bobby Hathaway is still a dedicated Space Corps employee."

"He's no longer a captain of a ship. And he never will be again."

"Right. Mommy got him a cushy desk job back at Space Corps Headquarters."

The silence was deafening and it made Eve want to kick something.

"I'm sorry, Eve. We all know what happened wasn't right."

Eve jerked on her chains and they clanked against the chair. "And you let it happen. All of Space Corps leadership did, to appease Mommy Hathaway. I dedicated my life to the Corps, and you all screwed me over for an admiral's incompetent son. I got sentenced to prison for *his* mistakes." Stomach turning in vicious circles, Eve looked at the floor, sucking in air. She stared at the soft booties on her feet. Damned inmate footwear. She wasn't even allowed proper fucking shoes.

Admiral Barber moved to her side. "I'm here to offer you a chance at freedom."

Gaze narrowing, Eve looked up. Barber looked... nervous. Eve had never seen the self-assured woman nervous before.

"There's a mission. If you complete it, you'll be released from prison."

Interesting. "And reinstated? With a full pardon?"

Barber's lips pursed and her face looked pinched. "We can negotiate."

So, no. "Screw your offer." Eve would prefer to rot in her cell, rather than help the Space Corps.

The admiral moved in front of her, her low-heeled pumps echoing on the floor. "Eve, the fate of the world depends on this mission."

Barber's serious tone sent a shiver skating down Eve's spine. She met the woman's brown eyes.

"The Kantos are gathering their forces just beyond the boundary at Station Omega V."

Fuck. The Kantos. The insectoid alien race had been nipping at Earth for years. Their humanoid-insectoid soldiers were the brains of the operation, but they encompassed all manner of ugly, insect-like beasts as well.

With the invention of zero-point drives several decades ago, Earth's abilities for space exploration had exploded. Then, thirty years ago, they'd made first contact with an alien species—the Eon.

The Eon shared a common ancestor with the humans of Earth. They were bigger and broader, with a few differing organs, but generally human-looking. They had larger lungs, a stronger, bigger heart, and a more efficiently-designed digestion system. This gave them increased strength and stamina, which in turn made them excellent warriors. Unfortunately, they also wanted nothing to do with Earth and its inferior Terrans.

The Eon, and their fearsome warriors and warships, stayed inside their own space and had banned Terrans from crossing their boundaries.

Then, twenty years ago, the first unfortunate and bloody meeting with the Kantos had occurred.

Since then, the Kantos had returned repeatedly to nip at the Terran borders—attacking ships, space stations, and colonies.

But it had become obvious in the last year or so that the Kantos had something bigger planned. The Haumea Incident had made that crystal clear.

The Kantos wanted Earth. There were to be no treaties, alliances, or negotiations. They wanted to descend like locusts and decimate everything—all the planet's resources, and most of all, the humans.

Yes, the Kantos wanted to freaking use humans as a food source. Eve suppressed a shudder.

"And?" she said.

"We have to do whatever it takes to save our planet."

Eve tilted her head. "The Eon."

Admiral Barber smiled. "You were always sharp, Eve. Yes, the Eon are the only ones with the numbers, the technology, and the capability to help us repel the Kantos."

"Except they want nothing to do with us." No one had seen or spoken with an Eon for three decades.

"Desperate times call for desperate measures."

Okay, Eve felt that shiver again. She felt like she was standing on the edge of a platform, about to be shoved under the starship again.

"What's the mission?" she asked carefully.

"We want you to abduct War Commander Davion Thann-Eon."

Holy fuck. Eve's chest clenched so tight she couldn't even draw a breath. Then the air rushed into her lungs, and she threw her head back and laughed. Tears ran down her face.

"You're kidding."

But the admiral wasn't laughing.

Eve shook her head. "That's a fucking suicide mission. You want me to abduct the deadliest, most decorated Eon war commander who controls the largest, most destructive Eon warship in their fleet?"

"Yes."

"No."

"Eve, you have a record of making...risky decisions."

Eve shook her head. "I always calculate the risks."

"Yes, but you use a higher margin of error than the rest of us."

"I've always completed my missions successfully." The Haumea Incident excluded, since that was Bobby's brilliant screw-up.

"Yes. That's why we know if anyone has a chance of making this mission a success, it's you."

"I may as well take out a blaster and shoot myself right now. One, I'll never make it into Eon space, let alone aboard the *Desteron*."

Since the initial encounter, they'd collected whatever intel they could on the Eon. Eve had seen secret schematics of that warship. And she had to admit, the thought of being aboard that ship left her a little damp between her thighs. She loved space and flying, and the big, sleek warship was something straight out of her fantasies.

"We have an experimental, top-of-the-line stealth ship for you to use," the admiral said.

Eve carried on like the woman hadn't spoken. "And two, even if I got close to the war commander, he's bigger and stronger than me, not to mention bonded to a fucking deadly alien symbiont that gives him added strength and the ability to create organic armor and weapons with a single thought. I'd be dead in seconds."

"We recovered a...substance that is able to contain the symbiont the Eon use."

Eve narrowed her eyes. "Recovered from where?"

Admiral Barber cleared her throat. "From the wreck of a Kantos ship. It was clearly tech they were developing to use against the Eon."

Shit. "So I'm to abduct the war commander, and then further enrage him by neutralizing his symbiont."

"We believe the containment is temporary, and there is an antidote."

Eve shook her head. "This is beyond insane."

"For the fate of humanity, we have to try."

"*Talk* to them," Eve said. "Use some diplomacy."

"We tried. They refused all contact."

Because humans were simply ants to the Eon. Small, insignificant, an annoyance.

Although, truth be told, humanity only had itself to blame. By all accounts, Terrans hadn't behaved very well at first contact. The meetings with the Eon had turned into blustering threats, different countries trying to make alliances with the aliens while happily stabbing each other in the back.

Now Earth wanted to abduct an Eon war commander. No, not a war commander, *the* war commander. So dumb. She wished she had a hand free so she could slap it over her eyes.

"Find another sacrificial lamb."

The admiral was silent for a long moment. "If you

won't do it for yourself or for humanity, then do it for your sisters."

Eve's blood chilled and she cocked her head. "What's this got to do with my sisters?"

"They've made a lot of noise about your imprisonment. Agitating for your freedom."

Eve breathed through her nose. God, she loved her sisters. Still, she didn't know whether to be pleased or pissed. "And?"

"Your sister has shared some classified information with the press about the Haumea Incident."

Eve fought back a laugh. Lara wasn't shy about sharing her thoughts about this entire screwed-up situation. Eve's older sister was a badass Space Corps special forces marine. Lara wouldn't hesitate to take down anyone who pissed her off, the Space Corps included.

"And she had access to information she should not have had access to, meaning your other sister has done some...creative hacking."

Dammit. The rush of love was mixed with some annoyance. Sweet, geeky Wren had a giant, super-smart brain. She was a computer-systems engineer for some company with cutting-edge technology in Japan. It helped keep her baby sister's big brain busy, because Wren hadn't found a computer she couldn't hack.

"Plenty of people are unhappy with what your sisters have been stirring up," Barber continued.

Eve stiffened. She didn't like where this was going.

"I've tried to run interference—"

"Admiral—"

Barber held up a hand. "I can't keep protecting them,

Eve. I've been trying, but some of this is even above my pay grade. If you don't do this mission, powers outside of my control will go after them. They'll both end up in a cell right alongside yours until the Kantos arrive and blow this prison out of the sky."

Her jaw tight, Eve's brain turned all the information over. *Fucking fuck.*

"Eve, if there is anyone who has a chance of succeeding on this mission, it's you."

Eve stayed silent.

Barber stepped closer. "I don't care if you do it for yourself, the billions of people of Earth, or your sisters—"

"I'll do it." The words shot out of Eve, harsh and angry.

She'd do it—abduct the scariest alien war commander in the galaxy—for all the reasons the admiral listed—to clear her name, for her freedom, to save the world, and for the sisters she loved.

Honestly, it didn't matter anyway, because the odds of her succeeding and coming back alive were zero.

EVE LEFT THE STARSHIP GYM, towel around her neck, and her muscles warm and limber from her workout.

God, it was nice to work out when it suited her. On the Citadel Prison, exercise time was strictly scheduled, monitored, and timed.

Two crew members came into view, heading down the hall toward her. As soon as the uniformed men spotted her, they looked at the floor and passed her quickly.

Eve rolled her eyes. Well, she wasn't aboard the *Polaris* to make friends, and she had to admit, she had a pretty notorious reputation. She'd never been one to blindly follow the rules, plus there was the Haumea Incident and her imprisonment. And her family were infamous in the Space Corps. Her father had been a space marine, killed in action in one of the early Kantos encounters. Her mom had been a decorated Space Corps member, but after Eve's dad had died, her mom had started drinking. It had deteriorated until she'd gone off the rails. She'd done it quite publicly, blaming the Space Corps for her husband's death. In the process, she'd forgotten she had three young, grieving girls.

Yep, Eve was well aware that the people you cared for most either left you, or let you down. The employer you worked your ass off for treated you like shit. The only two people in the galaxy that didn't apply to were her sisters.

Eve pushed thoughts of her parents away. Instead, she scanned the starship. The *Polaris* was a good ship. A mid-size cruiser, she was designed for exploration, but well-armed as well. Eve guessed they'd be heading out beyond Neptune about now.

The plan was for the *Polaris* to take her to the edge of Eon space, where she'd take a tiny, two-person stealth ship, sneak up to the *Desteron*, then steal onboard.

Piece of cake. She rolled her eyes.

Back in her small cabin, she took a quick shower, dressed, and then headed to the ops room. It was a small room close to the bridge that the ship's captain had made available to her.

She stepped inside, and all the screens flickered to life. A light table stood in the center of the room, and everything was filled with every scrap of intel that the Space Corps had on the Eon Empire, their warriors, the *Desteron*, and War Commander Thann-Eon.

It was more than she'd guessed. A lot of it had been classified. There was fascinating intel on the four Eon homeworld planets—Eon, Jad, Felis, and Ath. Each Eon warrior carried their homeworld in their name, along with their clan names. The war commander hailed from the planet Eon, and Thann was a clan known as a warrior clan.

Eve swiped her fingers across the light table and studied pictures of the *Desteron*. They were a few years old and taken from a great distance, but that didn't hide the warship's power.

It was fearsome. Black, sleek, and impressive. It was built for speed and stealth, but also power. It had to be packed with weapons beyond their imagination.

She touched the screen again and slid the image to the side. Another image appeared—the only known picture of War Commander Thann-Eon.

Jesus. The man packed a punch. All Eon warriors looked alike—big, broad-shouldered, muscular. They all had longish hair—not quite reaching the shoulders, but not cut short, either. Their hair usually ranged from dark brown to a tawny, golden-brown. There was no black or blond hair among the Eon. Their skin color ranged from dark-brown to light-brown, as well.

Before first contact had gone sour, both sides had done some DNA testing, and confirmed the Eon and Terrans shared an ancestor.

The war commander was wearing a pitch-black, sleeveless uniform. He was tall, built, with long legs and powerful thighs. He was exactly the kind of man you expected to stride onto a battlefield, pull a sword, and slaughter everyone. He had a strong face, one that shouted power. Eve stroked a finger over the image. He had a square jaw, a straight, almost aggressive nose, and a well-formed brow. His eyes were as dark as space, but shot through with intriguing threads of blue.

"It's you and me, War Commander." If he didn't kill her, first.

Suddenly, sirens blared.

Eve didn't stop to think. She slammed out of the ops room and sprinted onto the bridge.

Inside, the large room was a flurry of activity.

Captain Chen stood in the center of the space, barking orders at his crew.

Her heart contracted. God, she'd missed this so much. The vibration of the ship beneath her feet, her team around her, even the scent of recycled starship air.

"You shouldn't be in here," a sharp voice snapped.

Eve turned, locking gazes with the stocky, bearded XO. Sub-Captain Porter wasn't a fan of hers.

"Leave her," Captain Chen told his second-in-command. "She's seen more Kantos ships than all of us combined."

The captain looked back at his team. "Shields up."

Eve studied the screen and the Kantos ship approaching.

It looked like a bug. It had large, outstretched legs, and a bulky, segmented, central fuselage. It wasn't the biggest ship she'd seen, but it wasn't small, either. It was probably out on some intel mission.

"Sir," a female voice called out. "We're getting a distress call from the *Panama*, a cargo ship en route to Nightingale Space Station. They're under attack from a swarm of small Kantos ships."

Eve sucked in a breath, her hand curling into a fist. This was a usual Kantos tactic. They would overwhelm a ship with their small swarm ships. It had ugly memories of the Haumea Incident stabbing at her.

"Open the comms channel," the captain ordered.

"Please...help us." A harried man's voice came over the distorted comm line. "...can't hold out much...thirty-seven crew onboard...we are..."

Suddenly, a huge explosion of light flared in the distance.

Eve's shoulders sagged. The cargo ship was gone.

"Goddammit," the XO bit out.

The front legs of the larger Kantos ship in front of them started to glow orange.

"They're going to fire," Eve said.

The captain straightened. "Evasive maneuvers."

His crew raced to obey the orders, the *Polaris* veering suddenly to the right.

"The swarm ships will be on their way back." Eve knew the Kantos loved to swarm like locusts.

"Release the tridents," the captain said.

Good. Eve watched the small, triple-pronged space mines rain out the side of the ship. They'd be a dangerous minefield for the Kantos swarm.

The main Kantos ship swung around.

"They're locking weapons," someone shouted.

Eve fought the need to shout out orders and offer the captain advice. Last time she'd done that, she'd ended up in shackles.

The blast hit the *Polaris*, the shields lighting up from the impact. The ship shuddered.

"Shields holding, but depleting," another crew member called out.

"Sub-Captain Traynor?" The captain's dark gaze met hers.

Something loosened in her chest. "It's a raider-class cruiser, Captain. You're smaller and more maneuverable. You need to circle around it, spray it with laser fire. Its weak spots are on the sides. Sustained laser fire will eventually tear it open. You also need to avoid the legs."

"Fly circles around it?" a young man at a console said. "That's crazy."

Eve eyed the lead pilot. "You up for this?"

The man swallowed. "I don't think I can..."

"Sure you can, if you want us to survive this."

"Walker, do it," the captain barked.

The pilot pulled in a breath and the *Polaris* surged forward. They rounded the Kantos ship. Up close, the bronze-brown hull looked just like the carapace of an insect. One of the legs swung up, but Walker had quick reflexes.

"Fire," Eve said.

The weapons officer started firing. Laser fire hit the Kantos ship in a pretty row of orange.

"Keep going," Eve urged.

They circled the ship, firing non-stop.

Eve crossed her arms over her chest. Everything in her was still, but alive, filled with energy. She'd always known she was born to stand on the bridge of a starship.

"More," she urged. "Keep firing."

"Swarm ships incoming," a crew member yelled.

"Hold," Eve said calmly. "Trust the mines." She eyed the perspiring weapons officer. "What's your name, Lieutenant?"

"Law, ma'am. Lieutenant Miriam Law."

"You're doing fine, Law. Ignore the swarm ships and keep firing on the cruiser."

The swarm ships rushed closer, then hit the field of mines. Eve saw the explosions, like brightly colored pops of fireworks.

The lasers kept cutting into the hull of the larger Kantos ship. She watched the ship's engines fire. They were going to try and make a run for it.

"Bring us around, Walker. Fire everything you have, Law."

They swung around to face the side of the Kantos ship straight on. The laser ripped into the hull.

There was a blinding flash of light, and startled exclamations filled the bridge. She squinted until the light faded away.

On the screen, the Kantos ship broke up into pieces.

Captain Chen released a breath. "Thank you, Sub-Captain."

Eve inclined her head. She glanced at the silent crew. "Good flying, Walker. And excellent shooting, Law."

But she looked back at the screen, at the debris hanging in space and the last of the swarm ships retreating.

They'd keep coming. No matter what. It was ingrained in the Kantos to destroy.

They had to be stopped.

Eon Warriors

Edge of Eon

Touch of Eon

Heart of Eon

Kiss of Eon

Mark of Eon

Claim of Eon

Storm of Eon

Soul of Eon

King of Eon

Also Available as Audiobooks!

Want more action-packed sci-fi romance? Then check out the **Galactic Kings**.

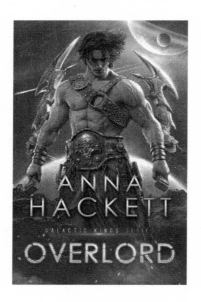

When an experimental starship test goes

horribly wrong, a test pilot from Earth is flung across the galaxy and crash lands on the planet of a powerful alien king.

Pilot Mallory West is having a really bad day. She's crashed on an alien planet, her ship is in pieces, and her best friend Poppy, the scientist monitoring the experiment, is missing. Dazed and injured, she collapses into the arms of a big, silver-eyed warrior king. But when her rescuer cuffs her to a bed and accuses her of being a spy, Mal knows she has to escape her darkly tempting captor and find her friend.

Overlord Rhain Zhalto Sarkany is in a battle to protect his planet Zhalto and his people from his evil, power-hungry father. He'll use every one of his deadly Zhalton abilities to win the fight against his father's lethal warlord and army of vicious creatures. Rhain suspects the tough, intriguing woman he pulls from a starship wreck is a trap, but when Mal escapes, he is compelled to track her down.

Fighting their overwhelming attraction, Mal and Rhain join forces to hunt down the warlord and find Poppy. But as Mal's body reacts to Zhalto's environment, it awakens dormant powers, and Rhain is the only one who can help her. As the warlord launches a brutal attack, it will take all of Mal and Rhain's combined powers to save their friends, the planet, and themselves.

Galactic Kings
Overlord

ANNA HACKETT

Emperor
Captain of the Guard
Conqueror
Also Available as Audiobooks!

ALSO BY ANNA HACKETT

Sentinel Security

Wolf

Hades

Striker

Steel

Also Available as Audiobooks!

Norcross Security

The Investigator

The Troubleshooter

The Specialist

The Bodyguard

The Hacker

The Powerbroker

The Detective

The Medic

The Protector

Also Available as Audiobooks!

Billionaire Heists

Stealing from Mr. Rich

Blackmailing Mr. Bossman

Hacking Mr. CEO

Also Available as Audiobooks!

Team 52

Mission: Her Protection

Mission: Her Rescue

Mission: Her Security

Mission: Her Defense

Mission: Her Safety

Mission: Her Freedom

Mission: Her Shield

Mission: Her Justice

Also Available as Audiobooks!

Treasure Hunter Security

Undiscovered

Uncharted

Unexplored

Unfathomed

Untraveled

Unmapped

Unidentified

Undetected

Also Available as Audiobooks!

Galactic Kings

Overlord

Emperor

Captain of the Guard

Conqueror

Also Available as Audiobooks!

Eon Warriors

Edge of Eon

Touch of Eon

Heart of Eon

Kiss of Eon

Mark of Eon

Claim of Eon

Storm of Eon

Soul of Eon

King of Eon

Also Available as Audiobooks!

Galactic Gladiators: House of Rone

Sentinel

Defender

Centurion

Paladin

Guard

Weapons Master

Also Available as Audiobooks!

Galactic Gladiators

Gladiator

Warrior

Hero

Protector

Champion

Barbarian

Beast

Rogue

Guardian

Cyborg

Imperator

Hunter

Also Available as Audiobooks!

Hell Squad

Marcus

Cruz

Gabe

Reed

Roth

Noah

Shaw

Holmes

Niko

Finn

Devlin

Theron

Hemi

Ash

Levi

Manu

Griff

Dom

Survivors

Tane

Also Available as Audiobooks!

The Anomaly Series

Time Thief

Mind Raider

Soul Stealer

Salvation

Anomaly Series Box Set

The Phoenix Adventures

Among Galactic Ruins

At Star's End

In the Devil's Nebula

On a Rogue Planet

Beneath a Trojan Moon

Beyond Galaxy's Edge

On a Cyborg Planet

Return to Dark Earth

On a Barbarian World

Lost in Barbarian Space

Through Uncharted Space

Crashed on an Ice World

Perma Series

Winter Fusion

A Galactic Holiday

Warriors of the Wind

Tempest

Storm & Seduction

Fury & Darkness

Standalone Titles

Savage Dragon

Hunter's Surrender

One Night with the Wolf

For more information visit www.annahackett.com

ABOUT THE AUTHOR

I'm a USA Today bestselling romance author who's passionate about ***fast-paced, emotion-filled*** contemporary romantic suspense and science fiction romance. I love writing about people overcoming unbeatable odds and achieving seemingly impossible goals. I like to believe it's possible for all of us to do the same.

I live in Australia with my own personal hero and two very busy, always-on-the-move sons.

For release dates, behind-the-scenes info, free books, and other fun stuff, sign up for the latest news here:

Website: www.annahackett.com

Made in the USA
Middletown, DE
21 March 2023